Eathan Davis is just a regular guy, he has grown up watching cartoons, and reading comics and books for most of his life, not to mention playing lots of video games.

He started writing for fun. Already doing his own online comics, he took a chance at writing a novel, not for fame or money but because he enjoyed it. His mind is unique and very bizarre so expect a lot of weird things to pop up every now and then.

This book is a first for him; it is like a passion for him to write new stories and create new worlds for his own enjoyment and everyone else's.

Eathan Davis

BOB'S WORLD

AUSTIN MACAULEY PUBLISHERS™

LONDON · CAMBRIDGE · NEW YORK · SHARJAH

A CIP catalogue record for this title is available from the British Library.

ISBN 9781528925280 (Paperback)
ISBN 9781528935760 (Hardback)
ISBN 9781528969307 (ePub e-book)

www.austinmacauley.com

First Published (2020)
Austin Macauley Publishers Ltd
25 Canada Square
Canary Wharf
London
E14 5LQ

I would like to thank my wife, Julie, for believing in me and encouraging me to go through with this book.

And I want to thank you, the reader, for reading this book; I hope you enjoy it as much as I enjoyed writing it.

Chapter 1

Carly Blake followed her mentor through the cold dark hallway, Wolfe leading the way as he followed the Warden and his assistant. The warden, old and grey as anyone with a bald spot going on his head, rubbing his forehead with a handkerchief as he stuffed it back in the breast pocket of his tweed jacket, his bowtie slightly damp.

His assistant is holding the clipboard, a young woman in her twenties with glasses hanging off her nose, twiddling a pen as she seemed nervous about this particular prisoner they are seeing, Carly could have sworn her name is Rebecca, or Rachel something with a R, she is not good at remembering names, how could she? She turned her head, moving her short black hair so she could look at Wolfe—the tall, gentlemen with a trench coat and a dirty tie, bald and shiny, mind you, as he was a proud African American man, why they were all the way in Australia she'll never know. She herself was wearing her favourite green trench jacket, over her Green Day shirt underneath.

'You sure you wanna see him?' said the Warden going to Wolfe.

'If the reason he's here is true, then I wanna know,' said Wolfe in that grunt, the Warden's been trying to change their minds all the way here, but Wolfe was adamant and refused to listen, unless he was a giant bat eating clown from Planet 9 he won't care. Carly wished she could go see a movie right now.

The assistant, Ruben, Ruby ah who cares, opened the hatch, the Warden hesitantly stepped in, with Wolfe and Carly followed suit, leading to a big empty space, in the middle is a locked glass box, big like a guy's living room, looked like it too as there was a couch, and a huge flat screen TV.

'Where did that TV come from?' asked Carly.

The assistant shook her head, 'We don't know, every day he seems to get a new thing, last time it was a swimming pool.'

Carly tried to picture a swimming pool in there, nope did not see it.

What she did see was the prisoner, wearing an orange jumpsuit with a dirty red shirt underneath as he sat on the couch, playing his PlayStation 4, so he got a PlayStation in there, how come the guards did not notice? She would have definitely noticed a prisoner moving a huge TV in there.

The prisoner seemed to ignore his new visitors, Carly looked closely at him, he looked like a dag, short spiky brown hair and a beard covering his chin, a typical Aussie as the warden described him. Speaking of which the Warden came up to a door, to the intercom as he spoke. 'Prisoner 213, you have visitors,' he said weakly.

'Tell them to get lost!' he said mashing buttons.

Wolfe decided to speak, moving the warden. He pushed the button, 'Mr Stewart, I am John Wolfe of Haven, I would like a moment of your time.'

'Sorry, I must have been rude before,' he said as he turned to face them.

'Get the holy hell out of my face!' he smiled as he turned back, then added 'pretty please.'

This guy was irritating, thought Carly as she resisted the urge to go in there and slap him a new one.

'I noticed you got a TV in there, playing Overwatch?' asked Wolfe.

'Dragon Ball Xenoverse,' he replied.

'Ah, the guy with that straw hat.'

'That's One Piece, what do you want?' he finally paused it as he looked at him.

Wolfe stared at him, not moving an inch as the prisoner got up and walked to the edge, until he is face to face with him, 'I wanna know how a killer just walked out of his cell, got a TV, PlayStation and some comic books by his bed, and walked back in,' he said.

'With these,' the prisoner pulled out the keys out of his pockets.

Both the Warden and the assistant gasped, 'Where did you get that?!' he yelled pointing to the keys in his hands.

'First day when I got here.'

'Those are the missing keys!' said the assistant, 'We have been searching for those, but we never found them!'

'Which means you have come and gone for the past three years you have been here,' said Wolfe, 'Why did you not escape and never come back?'

'Well, it's 'cause I'm innocent,' he said putting the keys back in his pocket. 'And for the record I never used them anyway, so you can have them back,' he chucked it at the door to the glass cell, hitting the glass with a clank and fell on the ground.

'You killed a girl,' Wolfe continued, the Warden and the assistant squabbling behind him which he just ignored, while the prisoner kept his own eyes on his.

'I did not kill her.'

'So, tell me what happened?'

The prisoner glared. 'Haven't you read the report, old man?' he grunted getting sick of this conversation like he had it many times before.

'I did, but I wanna hear it from you.'

The prisoner smirked. 'Nah, not gonna bother,' he said turning away and heading back to the couch, 'I'm sure the Warden can show you the door, if not it's down past A block and through Z block,' he added making the Warden squabble more as he sat back on the couch.

The nerve of this guy, Carly sighed, guess he's not budging, but Wolfe wasn't giving up, he pushed the button on the panel to open the glass door and walked right in the cell. 'Hey, what are you doing?!' yelled Carly as the door got slammed in front of her, stopping in place as she put her hands on the glass, what the hell was he up to?

'Mr Wolfe, it's dangerous in there!' yelled the Warden pushing the girl away, going to push the button to get in but he hesitated, thinking it's best to wait for the guards.

But Wolfe ignored him, standing by the couch the prisoner stood back up. 'Got something to say?' he said, ''Cause I hear it's dangerous being on the other side of the door,' he looked at him, getting ready for a fight, 'After all, I am a dangerous serial killer, literally anything here is my weapon.'

Wolfe chuckled. 'Are you a gambling man, Mr Stewart?' he asked, hands in his pockets to give off an air of confidence. He was a man with a mission and no matter what, Wolfe always comes out on top that is just what Carly always believed.

The prisoner took a step as he stood casually. 'I gamble when I know I'm gonna win,' he said, 'Otherwise, it's a waste of time,' he put his own hands in his pockets, mimicking the stranger. 'What do you have in mind?' he asked, curiosity getting the better of him.

Wolfe smiled, 'Well, how about a friendly wager, I bet that you'll be sitting in what remains of your bed, beaten and at my mercy,' he told him pointing to the bed by the corner

The prisoner glared at him. 'Really now? Well, I bet you'll be on the ground with my boot on your broken nose,' he said returning the gesture, 'That's how this will end, so what will happen then?'

'If you win, I'll leave, you will never see me or my apprentice again,' he took his hands out, 'You can live out your sentence of what, ten, twenty years left I think, in peace or whatever you do in your spare time,' The prisoner took his hands out, getting ready he clutch them tight, 'But if I win, and let's face it I never lose, You will come with me to hear out a proposition.'

'Give me a break,' he just muttered.

'So, do we have a deal?'

'Fine, but I strike first.'

The prisoner launched forward, sending a right hook straight at Wolfe's face, Wolfe dodged back, missing so easily, Carly knew this will be a quick fight seeing this guy had no training and no idea what he's up against, but he did know to send a roundhouse kick straight after his punch knocking Wolfe back to the wall. Wolfe coughed, catching his breath but the prisoner grabbed his collar, one hand on his side he lifted him over his shoulder and slammed him into the ground. The Warden screamed for him to stop while the assistant covered her eyes, but Carly watched this prisoner slam his boot onto his face, breaking his nose with a loud crack that echoed around the room. At that point, the assistant fainted by the sound.

Wolfe looked up from the blood around his face, under his boot as the prisoner put his hands into his pockets, acting like the battle is over, 'I won, now get lost, will ya!' he said looking down.

'Well, he's a dead man,' Carly sighed, folding her arms.

The Warden looked at her, 'Don't you have any concerns for your mentor? He's lucky he did not get killed,' he then dabbed his forehead with his handkerchief.

'Yeah, I wasn't talking about him.'

In an instant Wolfe grabbed his leg, the prisoner looked down as he had seen the tiny electric streams rolling around his hand, before he could say anything he was then lifted into the air and flung to the side, hitting the couch with his head he left a dent. Wolfe flew up, yes, flew as in he levitated off the ground. Spinning to his side, he threw the prisoner across the cell with enough force to slam him like a sledgehammer into the bed, the bed smashing upon impact with wood and splinters bursting everywhere, leaving the prisoner to groan as he sat up back against the wall, in what remains of his bed, as Wolfe stood over him.

'I won,' he said.

The prisoner glared up at him. 'Fine, what is this proposition?' he said giving in, guess he was a man of his word after all.

'Well, you and I are going to leave this cell, go to that nice café down the street then you will hear what I have to say, and I think you will say yes,' he said turning to the door, 'But whether you refuse or not, either way you are now a free man.'

'Wait, what?'

'Wait, what?!' yelled the Warden slamming his hand on the wall, 'You can't do that!'

'OK, did you smoke a joint before coming here?' the prisoner replied ignoring the screaming guy on the wall, 'After my crimes and my sentence, not to mention your damn nose, you are seriously going to let me walk away?'

'Not before a moment of your time, privately,' he finished walking out the door.

The prisoner took a moment, thinking about this and how it could screw him over, but the way he saw it, this could be a chance to be a free man but he knew there was always a price. Standing up he dusted down his jumpsuit. 'Deal,' he said walking following him out of the cell, Carly got it open as they walked out, the Warden getting as far as he could from the prisoner.

'Mr Wolfe, this is going against the law and process of the justice system…' he stuttered going up to the strange man, 'He killed a girl of a high-class family, they will not let this one slide.'

'Tell them to take it up with me,' he just said pushing him away, 'Let's go Carly,' he gestured to Carly to walk too, which she followed but still keeping her eyes on the convict that they just let walked out.

The prisoner ignored the Warden blabbing behind them, leaving the building they made their way to the front gate, he turned to Wolfe. 'So how did you do that throw back there? I had you under my foot, but you flew and chucked me to the bed,' Wolfe chuckled, 'Just who are you guys?'

'All will be revealed to you,' he just said, 'Right now let's get to that café, I heard they make the best bacon in town.'

'So, do we get an introduction from you?' Carly said to the prisoner, looking smug so he knew that she wasn't the one to mess with as well.

He just grunted, 'Did you not read the report?'

She shrugged, 'Just your last name, did not mention anything about a first.'

'That's because you weren't paying attention,' said Wolfe.

'Hey, I was busy with other stuff…' she trailed off, that other stuff is Angry Birds related.

Wolfe chuckled. 'This is Carly, my apprentice in training, as you can see, she is as childish as the next one,' he added.

'Hey!'

'Apprentice for what?' said the prisoner.

'All in good time, have some patience,' he pulled out a cigarette, lighting it up to take a puff as the guards opened the gate, allowing them to leave.

Carly followed behind next to the prisoner. 'So come on, what do we call you anyway?' she asked again, being an annoying brat.

The prisoner groaned, knowing she wasn't going to stop, he said, 'My name is Robert Stewart, but you can call me Bob.'

Chapter 2

The bell rang on the counter as Carly stood with the menu in her hands, Wolfe gave her the job to order them some food. 'Burgers,' he said, 'With extra bacon and maybe a small meal for Bob.'

'Why is it always me,' she sighed, going through it, being an apprentice, she was always stuck with the lame jobs like getting coffee, shining the car and ordering the food, as Wolfe said one time, 'I'm not paying money for garbage.'

She flicked through it, looking at the different types of food on this thing, but her eye caught the one that say Bacon Surprise. It listed the ingredients but did not say what the surprise exactly is.

'Hello, madame, what can I get you?'

Carly looked up at the cashier, a young boy, probably the same age as her, with hair filled with grease and pimples on his face, one pimple she swore just waved at her. 'Oh hi, yes I'm just wondering what is the Bacon Surprise?' she asked nicely, pointing to the item on the menu.

That is a good question, the Bacon Surprise is a mystery to all new customers, and regular customers for it is a once a month special, the cashier took an oath to never reveal the secret to anyone, not even to a pretty girl or a cop looking to book him for the surprise, seeing the gullible look on this girl's face, and the chance to overcharge her, he just calmly said, 'Well, that is the surprise,' with an air of coolness. Carly frowned, curious even more, no she had decided to order it just for the surprise, but something else caught her eye.

A waiter walked past the cashier, the sounds of bones cracking getting both her and the Cashier's attention, both could see he was holding a plate of bacon, figuring that this was the

Bacon Surprise she watched him take the plate to the customer sitting at the end of the bench. 'Bacon Surprise,' the waiter said.

'Ah! Finally,' said the Customer grabbing his utensils, this customer is a big man himself, of course that meant he's fat but say that to his face and he'll stab you with the fork, he just got on his break from work and he was too hungry for a decent meal.

Carly and the Cashier, knowing what will happen himself, watched the customer put the fork right into the bacon…

'SURPRISE!'

The waiter sent a mighty fist right into the customer's face, sending him flying face first into the booth behind, the customer cursed loudly as he stood, rubbing his sore chin with rage. 'What the bloody hell was that?!' he yelled across the café.

'The surprise,' replied the waiter.

'PUNCHING ME IN THE FRICKIN' FACE?!' his face turn beet red while he spat with bile.

The waiter nodded, 'It is on the fine print of the poster,' he pointed to the poster of the Bacon Surprise on the wall, underneath on the bottom in small print reads, 'We are not responsible for random punches to the face, as it is with your consent since you have bought the meal.'

'I demand to speak to your manager!' he yelled back

The waiter nodded, but as if on cue the manager came bursting out of a wall, a big bellied man clutching a spatula looking like the type of guy that will eat you in seconds. 'Who demands to see me?!' he bellowed out.

The customer, let's call him Tony, stood his ground. 'I demand a refund and an apology for your Bacon Surprise,' he said looking up at the scary looking chef, this guy had some guts, I tell ya.

The Chef smiled, 'Why certainly, come into my office,' he pulled out his hand to the open door on the side, 'And we shall talk about refunds,' the chef/manager seemed like a nice guy, smiling with veins on his forehead that look very sinister.

Tony smiled, fixing himself he walked into the room, the Chef followed behind as the door close behind them, locking it so it won't open, the label on the plate of the door clearly read "Beating Room".

Carly turned back to the Cashier, 'Yeah I'll take the three beef burgers,' she said, clearly seeing enough.

The Cashier sighed in failure, he accepted the cash and placed the order while Carly grabbed her number and headed back to her booth by the window.

She sat next to Wolfe, both sitting across from Bob, the prisoner they released who may or may not be a serial killer, mind you. Both men seemed to be in the middle of a staring contest, looking at each other with those deadly eyes, neither blinking. They had been getting stares from other customers, beside the Bacon Surprise punch, they were not interested and more worried about the man in the prison jumpsuit having a beer, and this café didn't serve beers.

'So, I got us burgers,' she started breaking the air.

'So, what do you people want?' said Bob, ignoring her like she wasn't even there.

Carly pouted, sitting back in her seat while Wolfe sipped his coffee, 'So tell us how you ended up in prison?' he asked, putting the cup down on the small plate.

'Not the point,' he grunted.

'Oh, I think it is, a young man, sixteen years old with his whole life ahead of him gets arrested for a murder, claims he was in a fight with another man who he claimed was the real killer, killed his friend and was about to kill him next until he, as in you,' he pointed to Bob, 'Beat him down in a fist fight, and from the look of the crime scene smashed him with a giant hammer that was never found but the cops did find the sword that kill that girl.'

Bob folded his arms, listening to the rest Wolfe continued, 'The cops looked around but they found no trace of this man or any evidence he was involved, so they arrested you and sentenced thirty years in prison,' he lit up another cigarette and took a puff, 'That was three years ago, which you have been coming and going since then,' he looked him in the eyes, putting out the cigarette on the ashtray, 'So why would a serial killer who could escape and leave without a trace, stay in prison? Unless he was an innocent man?'

'Good story,' said Bob, 'Why would it matter if I was innocent or not, you are not gonna believe me either way.'

'Actually I believe you.'

Carly spat out her drink, coughing she grabbed the napkins to wipe herself and the mess off, 'Well, I'll be damned,' was all

Bob said, 'So you also believe the part where he used some kind of magic?'

'Yes, that part interested me the most; you said he was wearing some kind of invincible armour?' Bob nodded, 'And he claimed he was a guardian?'

'Like he was a nutjob playing God, he had one of those egos.'

'So, it was you,' he finished.

Bob glared, looking a bit confused which was a first, he looked at Carly hoping she could make more sense than this old grunt, but Carly sighed herself, 'Years back, three years in fact a guardian went rouge, he defected from the guardians' job to watch over the balance between mortals and sorcerers, but he thinks that mortals are supposed to be enslaved and fear all magic so he went to Australia to start his conquest.'

'He started in Sydney, I was with a task force sent to bring him down, but when we got there we found him, broken, armour smashed in pieces and he was unconscious, we did not know who did it or why, until today,' Wolfe explained.

'Well, you're welcome, now you seem to know a lot about me but I know nothing about you,' said Bob leaning back, taking a sip of his beer.

Wolfe put out his cigarette, 'We are a part of an organisation of humans who know the dark side of our world, sorcerers, monsters, hell that fat happy thing that lives under your bed, we are formed to keep them from destroying our world by fighting back.' he held up his hand, showing him the electric current forming around his palm, 'We have trained to use Talents, special skills akin to magic that allows us to fight back, I am called a taskmaster, Carly here is my apprentice.'

'Hi,' she said in such a mocking tone.

'God, why me,' Bob mumbled, 'Well, I'm sure you're busy fighting Voldemort or whoever so good luck and send Potter my thanks,' he was about to get up but a bird landed on his shoulder, Bob looked as it was a small pigeon, pecking his head while it flew in the air, kept on pecking until he was back in his seat. 'Jesus, what the hell?' he said shooing it away, the pigeon flying around the café grabbing some guys burger and flying out the open door.

'Get back here you flying RAT!' the guy screamed, getting off his seat and bolted out the door, going after the bird that flew over the trees while Carly giggled.

'Yeah, that would be my talent.'

'Telling prick birds to peck people and rob their burgers?' he grunted.

'Controlling the animals.'

'Oh, 'cause why the hell not,' he sighed. 'So, what exactly are these talents, besides giving you super strength and animal speech,' he said getting back into his seat, crossing his arms as he gave them the glare again.

Wolfe took another sip, 'Well, the Sorcerers have always been behind the scenes, getting involved in mortal affairs and no one knows about them, well, except us,' he took a pause, 'A hundred years ago, mortals had begun training to use something to fight against them, a special magic that only mortals are capable of, the talents allowed us to use such simple abilities. It's sort of hard to explain but think of them as a simple magician trick, but the trick is actually real.'

'So, I can pull rabbits out of a hat?'

'That and many more that we normally do but enhanced,' Wolfe chuckled. 'Actually, I never actually tried that, but the first person who used the talent is a man named Billy Old Bane,' he explained, 'Once the sorcerers discovered what he can do they tried to purify him, but he fought back and taught many more about it.'

'Now the talent can be taught or it can be awakened, say by doing the same habit or trick for a long time, Carly here enjoys the company of animals, so it's obvious that she has gained the talent of control over their minds.'

'I see, well, this has been a great history lesson, but I think we are getting off track,' Bob said leaning closer, his arm on the table now, 'So tell me about these guardians,' the thought of the crime still in his mind that he needed to know exactly what he was up against.

Wolfe grabbed a folder from his coat and spread it on the table, photos and reports came sliding out in front of him, 'The guardians are the watchers of the balance between magic and mortals, it is their duty to make sure either side doesn't acquire the ultimate power over the other,' he then added, 'They have ancient magic at their command, magic so ancient that no other sorcerer has the abilities they have,' Bob picked up a photo of an ancient tablet showing eight robed guys around a sun, 'We have been keeping tabs on them in secret, our organisation have a duty to protect all mortals, seeing as we're mortals ourselves, from great threats like this,' Bob moved to the next photo showing the imprisoned guardian, the man who made his life hell, 'That is the eighth guardian, the one you already took care of.'

'Kald,' read Bob.

Wolfe nodded, 'We got word that the guardians have grown tired seeing mortals ruin the world they have sworn to protect, thus they began to form a plan to murder all the mortals with one spell, we at Haven have no experience in fighting them but you do,' he added, pointing a finger at him, 'Which is why we need you to fight with us, with you on our side we might stand a chance against them, the fate of the world depends on it.'

Bob dropped the photos, 'I'm not a weapon you can use in your war, go find someone else to fight your battles,' he stood up, 'So are we done here? 'Cause my answer is no.'

'You do realise how serious this is.'

'I don't care, if you wanna fight gods or wizards, then be my guest, but I want nothing to do with you or your organisation,' he stepped out of the booth, 'Thank you for bailing me out, but like you said I can decide where I go from now on.'

Carly regretted not getting him the Bacon Surprise, Wolfe went to a lot of trouble to find him but he is being a complete jackass! Well, fine, they don't need him anyway. In fact, she did not believe that he did beat a guardian in the first place, these guys were very powerful so something as dumb as a street fight wouldn't keep them down. Wolfe sighed, 'I was hoping you would jump at the chance for an adventure, to save the world and avenge your friend.'

'Don't use her death as an excuse, revenge isn't going to bring her back or fix my life,' he growled.

'Your food has arrived,' said the waiter coming over to them, his bones cracking with each step while he held the tray, Carly took a look at him and *oh my God,* he was so skinny! She could clearly see the outline of his bones. *Forget them, give the food to him; he seriously needs it!* The waiter put each of their plates in front of them, ignoring the return of the deadly staring contest between Wolfe and Bob. He put "Beef Burger" in front of Bob and another "Beef Burger" in front of Carly and then he put "Bacon Surprise" in front of Wolfe.

Carly quickly looked to the plate and back at him, 'Wait we did not…'

The waiter punched Wolfe across the cheek, sending him through the shattered window upon impact, Bob cursed as he stood up, Wolfe was sprayed on the concrete not moving, Carly got up to face the waiter but he grabbed her hair and pulled it with all his force to smash her face into her food, it had hit so hard it drew blood down her head as he pulled back.

'My, my, not so strong are you, mortals? But aren't you supposed to be the so-called elite?'

Carly looked at his face, the face of a bone man smiling at her, 'You are…' her eyes turned to the photo on the table, staring at one of the faces of the guardians who had the exact same bone face.

'One of the guardians, Drybon,' he said holding her up, 'You did not think we would keep tabs on you? You stupid mortals,' he gave a great big sigh, 'Such is the way of course, you knock a mortal down…' A rock charged with talent shot into his head, Drybon's head tilted with a new hole shot deep in his skull, his bulging eyes turned to Wolfe outside, pieces of glass dug into his skin drawing so much blood that it dribbled down his clothes. 'They think they can get back up,' he finished making cracking sounds with his neck while the bone grew back to close off the wound, he had drawn no blood, 'But my bones can regenerate AND grow back,' he held out his hand to him, finger nails aiming straight at him.

The nails burst open, as the tip of his finger bones shot out like bullets through the window shooting Wolfe even more that he was blown back into a car, setting off its alarm. At that point, people started to run from the café, screaming and yelling they ran from the crazed maniac shooting up the place.

Drybon laughed. 'YES RUN! RUN YOU COWARDS!' he yelled out laughing at all the chaos that the mortals make, some are pushing each other to the floor, the manager swinging a bat at everyone just to make it out of the window, Carly tried to send a high kick to his face but he moved his head back to bend it in such a way it looked like he was the crooked man. 'Nice try, darling,' He said moving his head back then he used great strength to smash her face again right into the side of the booth. Carly spat out blood her vision is fading, the chef and his workers ran with the customers out the door, Drybon laughing as he was going to kill them all, they just couldn't win against a guardian.

Her vision turned black, the last sight she could see was that jackass standing in front of Drybon.

Drybon's laugh rang through the abandoned café, his objective almost completed for he would end the lives of those two humans who thought they could stop what could not be stopped, like a mouse fighting the shotgun-wielding elephant! Oh, how he admired the screams of humans, hearing the mortals running to escape the cruel fate he had in store for them but it's no matter for they will be dealt with later.

But the sour note in his sympathy is this human, a prisoner from some prison he did not care, but what he did care was that that human wasn't running nor did he look scared or intimidated, just standing there with his hands in his pockets, giving him a dirty glare.

'Hello police! There is this man here attacking people, please send help!' Drybon turned his head 180 degrees to see a man, a businessman here for his daily lunch break calling the police on his phone and hiding behind the side of the counter, smiling he winked at him, sending a tiny cheekbone to shoot through the phone and into his throat. The man choked on his own blood, dropping the phone he fell face forward right into a pool of his own blood foaming under him. Drybon smiled, oh, he loved the smell of a mortal blood, made him feel alive but he turned back to the one human giving him a dirty look, he did not show any sign of fear. Hell, he looked even angrier just by watching what he did.

The girl was knocked out cold in his hand, her teacher dying unconscious outside, all he had to do was to kill them and his job was done but he just did not like the look this human was giving him, he should be feared! Worshiped! Hell, this human should be begging for his pathetic life! He just killed one of them for fun!

'Stop giving me that, LOOK!' he commanded.

The human did not budge. 'We were having a conversation,' he said, 'So, it was rude of you to knock him out the window, mind you I was close to doing it myself.'

Drybon laughed. 'Oh I see, well, I'm just gonna kill them quickly, BUT if you want I will kill you next, just give me a minute,' he said raising the girl up, he extended a long bony figure towards her eye sockets, planning to poke out her eyes to get to her brain.

'Put her down.'

Drybon turned to him with a loud crack, the human reaching behind his back going for a pocketknife. 'Oh? Well, who the hell are YOU to demand such things from a guardian?' he chuckled, holding the girl down to his leg as he prepared his bones, the human should've known that stabbing him won't do any good, his bones were as hollow as a tree so once he pulled the knife out he would attempt to stab him in the chest, leaving him open for his hand to grab his head and send a barrage of bones through his skull; blowing like a machine gun right through his head at close range. He could almost taste the blood seeping out everywhere from his eyes and mouth. OH, how it will be glorious in real life!

Drybon smiled, getting ready for the human to begin his attack and pull out his...

AK-47.

Drybon wailed as the barrage of bullets shot into him, speeding through his hollow bones and making a whistling sound but it was a silent cry compared to the loud banging, the AK was making in the human's hands, shooting all the bullets he had, right into him. Sure, the bullets won't do anything but shooting through his bones still HURT LIKE HELL!

The click of the empty barrel filled the silence of the cafe, the human dropped the gun and kicked it away, he prepared himself for the next attack 'Cause, of course, he knew a gun won't do anything to a guardian. But it did make him mad and that was his intention. Drybon stood up, smoke emitting from his bullet wounds but with no muscle or blood to bleed, he was still standing. 'You bastard,' he said through gritted teeth, 'I will make you pay for that!'

The human held up his right hand, moving his fingers together to make the gesture "Bring it".

Drybon smiled, holding his hand behind his head, he aimed his elbows towards him. 'Don't blink,' he said to him, opening his skin, so his humorous bones could shoot towards him. It was so fast that the human tried to block with his arms covering his head, one missed his head by mere inches but the other impaled his left arm going through it as it stuck out on the other side. He grunted in pain that he fell to his knee, he grabbed the end and pulled it out of his arm, a burst of blood spew forth and ran down his arm. Seeing it the human easily crushed the bone apart in his hand, looking at the shattered pieces remains falling to the ground.

Drybon chuckled while his humorous bones regrew. 'That is a lot of blood, and I DON'T think you'll last long now human,' he mocked.

'Just give me a minute, will ya,' the human muttered ripping off a sleeve and using it to wrap a make shift bandaged around the wound, tightening it so it can heal.

Drybon smiled his boney smile. 'Yes, keep that tough guy act up, makes it ALL the most delicious when I rip you apart,' he held out his arms again with his fingers held together pointing towards him. The human knew what's coming but it was too late, both hands shot out of the arms, coming at him like boney claws towards his face. The human bent backwards like he was at a limbo contest and missed them by an inch.

Drybon let out a screaming laugh as his hands grew back, he sent out the barrage of bones again while he was off guard, The human jerked back and rolled to the side, getting up to his feet he moved out of the way, jumped over the counter of the bar to hide behind it but already the bones pierced his shoulder arm and side, sending his blood to splatter on the wall behind while he fell behind the safety of the bench. 'That won't SAVE you!' sang Drybon focusing on the one spot of the bench that he hid behind and sent his bones right through it screaming with joy while the human was getting butchered. 'Yes! YES! DIE YOU PATHETIC WORM DIE!' he screamed sending all his bones until the bench forms into a pin cushion that got smashed and stabbed by a roller and sent through the meat grinder itself.

He stopped. Bones re-growing at the fingertips he had begun to laugh. 'So much for THAT attitude,' he said stepping towards the destroyed bench, giggling to himself he began to wonder what he might look like now, did he look like those dead pigs hanging in the cold room? Or was he a pile of meat now? Drybon could not wait but he wanted to savour this moment so he took his time, the girl and the taskmaster could wait.

He peered over the counter, trying hard not to laugh for he must enjoy all the sights he was seeing, he looked to the blood splattered wall by his bone barrage, oh how that must have hurt but the real show was just below, looking now to the open cellar door underneath it. The hatch was completely destroyed with his bones marking every broken wood and splintered pieces lying around, it was a sight to behold…

Open cellar door?

Running footsteps could be heard behind him, he turned his head in that same 180 degrees to see the human running towards him from outside the window, he took a step on the shattered ledge and another on the table, jumping off it to send a kick right into his spine. Drybon let out an ear-popping scream throughout the café, his spine had snapped in half making him fall backwards onto the ground, his head still facing the wrong way so it looked so wrong for him to lean back on his front. He looked up at the human standing over him, his jumpsuit was stained with his own blood on his right side, tiny finger bones sticking out from his shoulder and arm, the loss of blood made him breathe more deeper but he still had the strength and anger left to finish him, Drybon noticed the spiked covered gloves on his hands, the tips sharp and pointy on the knuckles, seeing this he now knew what was going to happen next.

His spine could regrow but it needed a bit time for it to do so, giving the human a short window to attack him which he would clearly take advantage of, 'Hey, hey, if you LIKE that girl I'll spare her,' he said holding up the back of his hands. Drybon planned to get more time to heal, or better to turn his hands around to quickly aim the fingers at his skull.

'Not so powerful, are you? Seeing as you have one major weakness,' he said cracking his neck side to side.

Drybon stopped. 'Weakness?' he spat, 'How dare you THINK that I have such WEAKNESS!'

'You got no muscle mate, no blood or anything really to protect your fragile bones making them easy to break,' he told him, pointing a finger at him, 'You are as fragile as a glass cup that's about to get smashed into a million pieces.'

Drybon will not have this; this human did not speak down to him like he is beneath him, he had one last attack that would take a lot out of him but it's a guarantee to kill this human, he let out a blood curl scream as his back burst wide open. His ribs had turned as well and grew like spiked tendrils rising up from the dry hole in his chest then they sped towards the human with the intent on impaling him!

The human stood tall, raising his arms, he closed his fists and swung them into the ribs, breaking them into twos before they could touch him. Drybon yelled in extreme agony, those were his ribs that could still make him feel pain AND now it'll take longer for him to heal.

'I'm guessing you never tried that before otherwise you would've used it earlier,' he grabbed the guardian with his good arm, 'Sucks doesn't it, you kill innocent mortals but never had one that fought back before right,' he flung him into the air and sent a closed spiked covered fist straight into his jaw, his jaw breaking apart upon impact with teeth flying out the corner of his mouth. The human smacked him right into the open door of the "Beating Room".

Drybon hit the ground chest first, his head bobbing around like a bobble head. He tried to stand but he had moved so many bones in his body that his legs buckled under him, putting him on the back on his knees making his shins break under him. The human walked into the room and left the door hung open so the light could shine around him, making him a shadow of death to the guardian's eyes. His mind was going haywire, actually afraid of what he'll do to him. 'He…hey, honestly I'm JUST doing my job, you know how it is,' he began, hoping to get some mercy out of him, 'Just let me go and I promise to never go after that girl or that guy, you have my WORD!'

'That guy you killed was doing his job but you killed him without a second thought,' he said coldly, 'How can I trust you to keep your word when you literally yelled out blood and death five minutes ago.'

Drybon shivered; sweat pouring down his face now, 'Just-I-Please…' He made a break for the door but the human kicked him back, Drybon whimpered on the ground, 'I can make you a

GUARDIAN! YOU'LL be like us just please DON'T KILL ME!'

'You'll give me what I want, huh?' the human said.

'YES! Anything you want!' Drybon yelled out. 'I'll do it for you no matter WHAT!'

'I want you to shut up.'

All the guardian saw next was nothing but a barrage of spike covered fists pummelling him everywhere, the spikes digging deep into his skull, neck, back, arms, legs, anywhere and everywhere on his body. All his bones splitting apart and smashed like his ribs. The bones broken apart with loud cracks, his arms and legs kicked furiously by the human's boots, breaking in halves, all two hundred six bones inside his body were getting smashed into tiny pieces inside him. The human continued punching and kicking him, Drybon never had a beating this severe before in all hundred years of his life! He screamed in agony but soon shut up by one last punch smashed into whatever's left of his jaw, sending him to his side gasping; he did not have blood, only the shattered remains of all his bones filling his lungs, making him cough them up. The guardian gasped and wheezed, he was too broken and in too much pain to focus on healing.

Drybon lay there pummelled, beaten and close to death. The human walked out of the room and towards the booth where the girl is laying on the ground. He grabbed the girl and hoisted her over his good shoulder. She hung there like a ragdoll, with one arm over her to hold her in place the human began walking out of the café, the bell on top of the door signalled his leave.

'Powerful, my ass,' he grunted.

Chapter 3

Police sirens blazed around the Café, cops and detectives were around helping civilians with their injuries or shock, some too traumatised to speak while others are telling them what happened.

'Dude, this guy punched out this bloke through the window!'

'He killed that guy and injured that girl.'

'There was a criminal sitting there; I think he's partner in crime.'

'I saw a mongoose.'

The crime scene was locked with police tape surrounding the area so the police can do their work, taking blood samples from the booth where it started, to the blood on the walls, to the blood of the poor bystander lying dead in a pool of his own blood, not to mention the millions if not billions of bones lying about. The detectives were dumbstruck, some said all of those came from the same guy but that is impossible. The blood led to the "Beating Room", a conversation they'll have with the owner another time, and found it empty except for more discarded bones.

A man came waltzing in, a tall dark gentleman with sunglasses black as the deepest void covering his eyes, his coat flowed with each footstep as they echoed in the café, getting the attention of all the police looking at him.

The gentlemen stopped in front of the one cop in charge, Constable John, his name was, a portly man who looked like he could not out run a frog. He turned to the gentlemen, 'Excuse me, but have you any clearance to be here?' he demanded.

'Certainly,' said the gentlemen showing him a badge, Mr Red, his name is, the organisation he's with did not say as he moved it so quickly out of sight from the policeman.

Constable John blinked, 'Right, well, we got ourselves a pickle here,' he said pointing to the pickle on the floor, 'A dead body over there…'

'Get to the point, who is the perpetrator?' demanded Mr Red.

'Well, from the blood samples we have gotten, all signs seemed to point to Robert Stewart, a known serial killer that was imprisoned for manslaughter,' explained Constable John.

'Tell me about him.'

The constable dabbed his head, 'Well, three years ago he killed his friend, found her dead in an alleyway cut in half while he was standing over her with blood around him, the court sentenced him to fifteen years in prison.'

'So, how is he walking around? Surely, he could not have escaped with the local police force knowing about it.'

'Well, earlier this morning he was signed out and freed to walk by a stranger with higher payrolls then ours,' he said with a groan, clearly not liking his job right now, if criminals could walk free by permission from a higher up.

'Interesting,' he said gliding into the room, putting a finger to his chin as he inspected the damage done to this room soon turning his attention to the inside of the "Beating Room". Looking down at all the bones scattered everywhere but no sign of a body.

'Weird, ain't it?' continued the constable kicking some of the bones, 'they are all over the place yet we could not find who they belong to, seeing as the other body had all of his bones.'

'Where is he now?'

'Well, he's at the morgue; we'll alert his next of kin.'

'The convict.'

'Oh him,' He shrugged. 'Well, we put out an alert on an ambulance van, apparently to a witness he hijacked the ambulance once they gotten here and put two people inside then drove off,' he sighed to himself, 'We gotta find them before this Stewart guy does something, who knows what demons he has.'

Mr Red turned and left, cutting through the kitchen and past the boxes of meat and discarded food on the plates, he stepped out to the back with the constable calling out to him from behind back in the café but he ignored him and walked along the alleyway, following the trail of broken bones.

Mr Red continued walking for ten minutes until he turned to a dead end, where a disfigured body laid huffing and panting. Mr Red gotten closer and looked down at his former colleague, disfigured and deformed with bones sticking out everywhere under his skin, a foot bone in his head, ribs for feet and collar bones for legs and wrists, his fingers had the toe bones and his jaw a combination of both hands, skull and spine makes up what's left of his body. He looked up gasping for more air, his head still turned around and facing his own back, 'H*elp...me...*' he begged.

He crouched down. 'What happened to you, Drybon?' he said in a cold tone, 'Did you kill the taskmaster and his apprentice?'

Drybon barely moved his mutated arm, 'H*e did this to me...a human...*'

'Was it the taskmaster, Wolfe?' Drybon shook his head, 'The girl?' he shook again.

'*A...mortal...*' He gagged out some tiny bones.

'You let a mortal do this to you?' He put a hand on his face, gritting his teeth, 'You let a mortal beat you, was he working with Haven?'

'*He wasn't... Working with anyone.*'

'Was he the convict?' Mr Red asked one last time, Drybon nodded his head to answer. Mr Red stood up, thinking that whoever this convict was must be the same one that defeated their brother three years ago, setting them onto their quest in the first place.

Drybon grabbed his pants leg. 'Please brother, the human broke all my bones that I did not know what to heal first, so they all healed at the same time in horrible places!' he cried gasping.

'Tell me about this human.'

Drybon gasped, 'He is smart, he figured out my weakness and used it against me, but if you heal me, I won't lose to him a second time!'

Mr Red stood still. 'No you won't,' he just said. He looked down to the deformed man, 'You had one job, kill Wolfe and Carly but not only are they still alive, also you got beaten by a mortal,' he grabbed the rim of his glasses, taking them off, 'In failing that you have betrayed us and our mission,' Drybon screamed, letting go he crawled back and gasping faster as he stared into his eyes. He tried to yell but there was no air to escape from his bone filled lungs, then Mr Red looked at him.

There was silence, a cold air blowing through the alleyway for a single moment. Mr Red walked out soon after, dusting off his coat and putting his sunglasses back over his eyes, the prisoner having his attention now but the prophecy did not say anything about him, so who was this man? His footsteps echoed away, pondering his next move for he could not let anything stop him from his goal, the others would want revenge for Drybon.

In the alleyway, by the bins and cats looking for a free meal, laid a black, charred corpse, no eyeballs in his dark eye sockets; on the face of a deformed creature with his mouth opened in a silent scream.

Meanwhile, far away into the Australian outback where the cows roamed, where emus went and carjacked poor civilians. Driving along the barren road, parked an Ambulance Van.

The setting sun shined on Carly's eyes waking her up from her slumber. She clutched her head throbbing in pain as she sat up on the soft ground of an ambulance van, looking up at Wolfe on the carrier, all bandaged up and resting. Remembering the events in the café, Carly yelled and fell out of the back doors and landed on her bare arms on the hard, burning ground. She stayed on her hands and knees feeling the heat hit her full forced into her skin, 'Gawd it's HOT!' she yelled standing up and shaking her hands, head still fuzzy from the impact which falling out in a panic did not help it one bit. She turned and walked face first into the wall of the ambulance, screaming again, 'What the hell is that yelling?!' she turned to see Bob coming from the driver's seat, his arms bandaged up, his right was even more bandaged than the other, he walked to Carly with that annoyed look on him.

'Oh, of course,' he said.

Carly growled at him, 'Where are we? What happened at the café?'

'Calm down, I saved your lives, that's what happened,' he said walking to the back and looking at Wolfe, 'I got all the bones out of your mentor and bandaged you guys up, you took quite a beating to your head, I think you could have a concussion.'

'Could?'

'Should, would, the details don't matter.'

Carly touched the bandaged tied around her forehead, 'Thank you,' she mumbled, 'But what happened to the guardian? Last thing I remember was him attacking us and was going to kill us.'

Bob folded his arms, 'I kicked his ass and saved yours,' he told her, 'You should've mentioned that the guardians are after you guys, otherwise, I would've stayed in prison.'

Carly folded her arms, 'You expect me to believe you beaten a guardian? Did you kill him?'

'No, left him in whatever's left in that weird body of his, it wasn't a pretty sight,' he said turning back around. All Carly could think was how the hell was he still in his prison jumpsuit? It's like 50 degrees out here!

But then she started searching around hoping they weren't followed, ever since she was a little girl she read all about the guardians, about how powerful they are with their ancient magic, so hearing that this random bloke beat one and left him to suffer seemed so impossible for her mind to comprehend, 'It sounds so impossible,' she whispered.

'It's possible.'

She turned to see Wolfe climbing out of the van, his trench coat hung over his shoulders he stepped down and stood with them, 'It proves he was telling the truth, the guardians can be defeated and killed like any other person,' he turned to Bob, 'Since, you left him alive he probably told his brothers about you so you can expect they will be coming for you as well, and you can't take them alone,' he pulled out his hand, 'So you're stuck with us as we are stuck with you.'

Bob hesitated, 'You know I was a lot happier in prison, no talents or magic's or homicidal guardians after my head.'

'And I wanted to be a ballet dancer, but life gets to you once in a while.'

He sighed, 'Fine, but, after this you can get lost,' he took his hand and shook, trying to break his hand with Wolfe doing the same. Carly really did not wanna hang out with this psycho any longer than she likes but like Wolfe said they are in this together.

'So what's next? Now that we have the guardians after us, we don't exactly know what they want.'

'What do you know, Wolfe,' said Bob letting go, hands going into his pockets, 'You wouldn't go through with this in the first place if you did not know what the endgame is.'

Wolfe looked to his comrades and chuckled, 'Well, the guardians hate all mortals, it's no secret they blame us for all the wrongdoings of the past,' he explained, 'The brother that got defeated so easily was the last straw for them to take action, now they are going to free their first brother from his prison.'

'And how did the first brother get imprisoned?'

'Well, it was us at Haven, we locked him up so he wouldn't threaten the safety of our world, but the guardians did not agree, but they stayed out of it 'cause they have a duty to uphold, but of course Kald disagreed with it, it was the reason he went rouge,' he took a pause, 'His defeat at your hands was the cause for this.'

'So, it's my fault,' Bob said.

Wolfe nodded, 'Don't worry, it was bound to happen sooner or later but right now we must stop them for if they free their brother then it's the end for all mortals, The First's magic is so ancient he can kill anyone with a single thought.'

'That sounds really bad, how do we stop him?' Carly asked.

Wolfe grinned. 'We need to go to our Australian Headquarters, they have the key that can open the door to him, but it is disguised so well,' he said turning to the van.

'And let me guess, the entrance is in Australia?' called out Bob.

'Of course, Australia has both the heat and cold to generate a perfect path into a void, taskmasters used their talents to lock it so no one can get through,' he explained getting into the driver's seat, 'The key is the result of the talent used.'

'So why not destroy the key?'

'Impossible, it was created by the First as a way to escape, but the taskmasters snatched it before he used it, it can't be destroyed.'

Wolfe looked at them, 'The first guardian is locked up in a place untouchable by anyone, even the guardians but we have the key.'

'Well, of course, ''cause why make it easy for us,' he sighed getting into the passenger seat while Carly climbed into the back, closing the doors behind her while Wolfe started the van, 'So I'm assuming the guardians are after this key.'

'Aye, their magic isn't powerful enough to open the door, so they have been looking for the key ever since, our sources told us that they have discovered its location.'

'So, they're going to the hub,' Carly said from the back, 'We have to stop them.'

'The hub?' Bob asked.

'The name of our headquarters, we have them all around the world but the Australian one is what we need to get to,' Wolfe said, 'You are going to have one hell of an adventure.'

Mr Red stepped out into the hot Australian sun, all the guardians or what's left of them stood in front of the tower, where their brother was held in his prison. But they could not get him out without the key, they had tried using their ancient magic but they had no effect on the talent-enhanced prison.

All five guardians stood together in front of the door to the tower, the tower itself tall as the sky. Mr Red told his brothers the news of Drybon's death, how he was sadly killed by a mortal named Robert Stewart. He told them of his condition and how he begged for mercy, a disgrace among all guardians.

They took the news quite well; they bid their goodbyes and prayers so they could wish him a safe passage into the afterlife. Yes, I am kidding for they instead broke any and all the trees or rocks around them, even going so far as making new rocks and trees just so they could break them. They all wanted revenge but Mr Red stood calmly watching them. Soon he stopped them by reminding them of their cause to bring back their brother from his banishment. They listened but still this human could not go on living if he can kill one of them.

'That is true,' Mr Red said, 'But our brother comes first, the mortal is a threat, along with the taskmaster and the girl from the prophecy, we cannot let them interfere with our cause.'

They all nodded, 'We can deal with the mortals once our brother returned but we need the key,' he turned to his brother, a shadow figure with smiles and muscles as strong as the strongest man on earth, 'You know where the key is Mickle, retrieve it at once,' he said, 'Leave the mortals to us.'

Mickle grinned, 'You got it, brother,' he turned and walked out, Mr Red could trust him, he had never failed an objective and never will, for he was the invincible man; no bullet or gun or punch or magic could harm him. Mickle jumped away from the tower, opening a magic portal to his destination, he charged straight through it with violence on his mind.

Mr Red then turned to the next figure sitting on his rock with his musical instrument in his hands, playing a tune on his prized clarinet for the rats to hear its sweet sounds of the night. 'Mozart,' he said, 'Wolfe and Carly must be dealt with,' the musician stopped playing, 'Take care of them for me, will you?'

'Of course, Brother,' Mozart smiled and stood up, he turned and left while the rats scurrying around dropped dead, all because the music had stopped playing.

Chapter 4

'Oh god, turn it off,' Carly moaned in the passenger seat, her and Bob switched during the petrol stop, so now he was laying on the stretcher taking a nap.

Wolfe ignored her and turned the radio up. 'No music can beat the classics of Elvis,' he told her and started to sing along, '...*You ain't nothing but a hound dog...*' driving her even more insane.

Carly turned to Bob sleeping on his back, clearly asleep from the loud snoring. She turned back to the window and stared out at the dark night sky over the flat dry grass surface. 'We should find a motel to sleep tonight,' Wolfe said next to her taking a sip of alcohol.

'Great.'

Wolfe raised his eyebrow. 'Is something bothering you?' he asked, ''Cause I'm detecting a sound of sarcasm.'

'Nothing.'

'Carly, let me tell you about the time, I found myself in bed naked with a werewolf and a donkey...'

'OK, OK, fine,' she gave in, she hated hearing those weird stories that he used to get her talking, it's always being in bed with someone or something like just what kind of life did he live? 'It's Bob, I don't think we can trust him,' she finally said.

'I see.'

'How do we know he actually did beat that guardian? Or the one before and he is just another serial killer that WE let out,' she sat back, 'I just think we are making a huge mistake.'

Wolfe took a moment, chuckling to himself while he managed to miss some kangaroos hopping across the road, 'I can see your concern, his methods are incredibly extreme but he did save us from Drybon, otherwise, we wouldn't have this conversation ''cause we would be dead in a morgue somewhere.'

'Yeah I know,' she sighed.

'Think of it this way, he could have run out of that café and left us, he did not know us nor does he care about our mission but instead he stayed and fought for our lives,' he took a look at her.

'He saved us.' Carly agreed.

'Exactly, if he really was a cold-blooded killer then why rescue us? Why not let him kill us that would solve all his problems,' he turned a corner as they reached a town, driving around the streets now, 'He fought the guardian, won and got us patched up while risking his freedom for two strangers he never met, that tells me that he has honour and that is what we need to win this war,' he pulled into a parking lot of a sleezy motel, getting out in front of the reception office so to check in.

The motel is small, with twenty-four rooms leading from the reception office and continued around the car park to the start of the entrance to the street. The walls were rotted, there was a police tape on one door and I think there's a bear living on the roof. The swimming pool was lime green so it would be best to avoid that area at all cost, mostly due to the mutated snakes living inside. So, if you're out in the country and need a place to rest, I suggest keep driving for it might just save your life.

Wolfe got back in holding the keys to Room 14 and 15, driving the van into the parking space for that room so he could get out and take a look around. Carly took a look at Bob in the back, thinking about what Wolfe said how Bob was now wanted by the guardians because of them yet he would still risk his neck, she gave a small smile but quickly hid it as Wolfe threw the back doors open and smacked his feet. 'Wake up! I got us a place to sleep for the night,' he told him.

Bob groaned, 'Great, where are we?' he climbed out of the van.

Carly got out from her side, looking at the two doors side by side, separate rooms for the three of them so who is going to share? 'I got us two rooms, seeing as Carly wants her privacy, we get to share room 15,' he told Bob handing her the key, 'We rest up, then head for the hub tomorrow.'

'I am not sharing a room with you,' said Bob.

'Too bad, we are not her parents so it would look bad that two grown men share a room with a teenage girl, we probably already have the law after us,' he told him.

'How about you sleep outside while I get the room to myself.'

'I was thinking you sleep outside instead; I need my beauty sleep.'

'So, does that mean you never sleep?'

Carly tried to hide a giggle while Wolfe gave him the bird, she always looked forward to having her own room, binge watching her favourite shows all night and have her favourite snacks, and she could not help but beam at the thought.

'Well, you two seem to have your sleeping arrangements settled,' she said unlocking her room and walking in, Bob already walking in the other room, 'Try not to kill each other before morning,' she teased.

'Hey Wolfe! There is only one bed!' Bob yelled from inside

'What?!' Wolfe turned sharply to look inside, 'I told them two beds! Those con artists lied to me! Hell, I gave them an extra hundred just to make sure!' he turned hoping to ask Carly to switch but too late she just waved and shut the door. Giggling to herself, she pictured them two awkwardly sharing the bed together.

She sat back on her bed with her phone in her hand, dialling to order a pizza for later tonight while she found the channel with the horror movies playing. She was going to enjoy that nice, peaceful night but was unaware of the danger that awaited just outside her door.

Wolfe laid awkwardly in bed with Bob lying next to him, both under covers and not saying one word while they stared at the ceiling.

'You know in some countries it's normal for two men to share a bed and not feel gay, hell we are lucky to have a bed this big while in poorer countries they only have the floor or rags to sleep on,' said Wolfe breaking the air.

'Yeah, well, not here,' said Bob, 'Here people get beaten up for that.'

Wolfe nodded, 'So any particular reason why you are sleeping in your prison jumpsuit?' he asked him, sure Wolfe was still in his shirt and tie but wearing a prison jumpsuit to bed is really putting it in the bizarre territory.

'Eh, not bothered changing just to sleep,' he replied.

'I see, well, we should try to get some sleep,' he said turning his back to him.

Bob just laid still, 'Wolfe,' he started, 'This place you are taking us, you say it's your headquarters?' he asked.

Wolfe yawned, 'Yeah, it was founded back in the 1800s, humans have discovered the supernatural world living among us so they formed Haven to train us to protect the people we love,' he closed his eyes, 'We have kept secret from the magical world, same as they kept a secret from us, we figured they should know how it feels.'

'Understandable, but that guardian back in Sydney, he was after you and the girl, why is that?'

Wolfe turned his head. 'I did not know you cared,' he mocked.

'I don't, but if they're coming after me, now, I would wanna know why,' grunted Bob.

He chuckled turning back, 'It's because of the prophecy.'

'Terrific,' he replied sarcastically, 'Now you have entered a cliché magic tale.'

'Laugh it up mate, recently a psychic has made a prediction about the guardians, the prophecy goes that a taskmaster and his apprentice will stop the guardians from wiping out the mortals, and with mine and Carly's track record they figured that we will be the ones to stop them but I find it all a bunch of crap,' he admitted.

'Why is that?' Bob sat up looking at him, 'I thought you people are all about prophecy, the chosen one and all that destiny stuff.'

'You read too many books you know that?' sighed Wolfe, sitting up himself, 'I don't believe it cause where in the prophecy does it say you?' he pointed to him, 'Where do you fit into this?'

Bob looked down. 'Well, you morons did involve me,' he said.

'Yes, we did, but you chose to stay, therefore the prophecy will not come true,' he lay back down, turning off the lamp, 'Do me a solid and don't tell Carly, this prophecy is what's kept her going.'

'What do you mean?'

Wolfe mumbled something in his sleep; his loud snoring filled the room leaving Bob alone laying back down as he thought about what he said.

Carly's eyes focused on the screen, the girl in the film was walking to the door of a cabin, taking a bite of her pizza, she watched the dumb as hell girl opening the door, 'Don't go in there,' she said, waiting for the moment that the killer showed up in the darkness and stabbed her right in the eye, 'Told ya,' she sighed, taking a sip of her drink while the movie continued with that stupid music playing. But then it hit a commercial, with the same music playing.

She raised an eyebrow, she switched the channel to another show but it had the same music, she turned the volume down until the TV was muted. The music was still going that she realised that it's coming from outside. She turned her head to the door, putting on her boots she opened the door to the warm air blowing in her face. 'Where is that music coming from?' she wondered.

She looked around the carpark until she stopped at a man playing a clarinet on the bench by the tree on the other side of the motel. He played his music into the night air that it seemed a little calming to hear, Carly noticed he was wearing a poncho, red and silver at the sides while he wore a red silver hat that went along with his outfit. His boots gleamed in the moonlight while he stood from the bench. One eye was opened so he could notice his new admirer walking towards him. He stopped playing the clarinet and held it at his side, but the music was still playing as if the musician isn't needed. 'Hello, madame,' he said in a cool velvet voice, bowing down and tipping his hat to her, Carly blushed at this chivalry. 'What a silent night we have,' he continued standing back up hat over his eyes but left one for her to see.

The music was still playing, sending out a tune that's almost enchanting to her with each step she took forward. 'Nice song,' she said keeping her cool, didn't know why this gentleman was so alluring to her.

The musician smiled, making her blush redder and smile wider, 'Why thank you, I play for the sweetest of gals,' he took her hand and made a small peck on the palm.

Carly pulled back her hand quickly. 'Oh, well, that's nice I guess...' she said, acting like a stupid schoolgirl who has a crush on the famous boy band or something.

The musician gave her the sweetest smile she had ever seen. 'That smile makes all the music to me,' he said enchanting her more with his voice, the music playing loud enough for Carly soon found herself in his presence, his finger under her chin lifting her gaze towards his. He looked into her eyes, her heart beating faster, she wanted to stay like this forever with this hunk of a man and she did not know his name.

'The name's Mozart,' he said in a calm voice, 'And I have found such a beautiful flower.'

'I...oh my...' she mumbled, fully mesmerised by his eyes she could stare into them forever.

'So, what's a pretty gal like you doing all the way out here?' he asked her gently.

'Well, hehe, I'm just on a mission,' she giggled pulling back, 'It's nothing special or anything,' she looked to the clarinet floating above them now, 'How are you doing that?' she asked him

'Magic, my dear,' Mozart told her holding his hand out to it, 'My music's magic plays the sweet sound of the clarinet without me having to use my fingers,' he explained to her.

'Wow!' was all she could say.

'So my beautiful flower, why don't you tell me everything that's inside that pretty head of yours,' he asked of her, gazing into her eyes while she gazed back, she did want to tell, she did want to do anything that made him happy, so she opened her mouth to form the words...

'OK, that's enough mate she's like half your age!'

A flash of anger surged through her, she turned sharply to look at Bob standing there with his hands in his pockets and that annoying glare on his face, 'Sorry to do this but I'm gonna have to break that instrument, Wolfe kicked me out to deal with that annoying music so you can understand I might get violent,' he took a step towards him but Carly charged right into him sending him to the ground, she had to protect him no matter what! She will not let Bob touch one finger on his perfect face so she punched his gut repeatedly, making him gasp out for air while she grabbed his arm and flipped him over so his face hit the ground. She got up back on her feet but left one foot on his back, 'What are you doing, you dumb brat,' he grumbled up at her flipping to his side in an attempt to lose her balance, but Carly jumped back and let him get back on his feet.

'I will not let you hurt him,' she said coldly, 'If you lay one finger on him, I'll tear that glare right out of your face,' she threw a punch to his abdomen, Bob swung back but she ducked, grabbed his arm and flung him over her shoulder so he hit the ground, holding his arm in a lock she twisted, making him scream.

Mozart's footsteps tapped on the ground, he walked up to Bob's eyesight so he could see him, 'My, my, so this is the human who killed my brother,' he took a sigh, 'Such a shame that you are going to be killed by one of your own.'

Deep in her mind she made the realisation that he is a guardian, but she did not care for she had made a vow to protect the man she loved.

The music from Mozart's Clarinet had its own special magic, by the tune it could enchant a young girl to fall madly in love, to making warriors turn on each other, either way Mozart was considered one of the dangerous guardians with this ancient magic.

'God damn it, I said go turn it off!' yelled Wolfe sitting up in bed, it was bad enough that Bob got the good comfy side of the bed but he could not even go kick that guy's head for playing his music on loud? Some criminal he turned out to be. Stepping out of bed he put on his shoes and coat, 'I swear if he left him alone on purpose just to tick me off...' he mumbled to himself walking outside to knock some heads around but he stopped at the doorframe shocked at the scene before him.

He stood there seeing Carly standing over Bob, arm in a lock with a musician, both seemed to have Bob on the ground unable to get up due to the strange strength, Carly seemed to have over him. 'I said don't give him that look!' Carly yelled pulling the arm, making Bob scream in pain. Wolfe ran towards them just as Bob pulled out a water gun from his front pocket and squirted Carly in the face so she could let go. Wolfe stopped just as Bob got back on his feet, chucking the water gun away.

'Oh, now you get up,' he mumbled looking at him.

Carly tried to dry her face with her shirt. 'That water was cold you jerk!' she yelled at Bob, but kinda grateful for the cool down during this heat. She stood in front of Mozart to protect him, going into a fighting stance.

'Yes, my darling, teach this rude cretin to respect those of higher class,' he said holding his clarinet, which was where the music was coming from. Wolfe trying to understand why Carly would listen to him, was it the music or his stupid hat?

'What the hell did you call me?' Bob tensed his fists ready to bash both their heads in, he then turned to Wolfe, 'Wolfe, he is a guardian,' he told him, 'He got your dumb protégée under some spell.'

'Of course,' Wolfe said smacking his head, 'He is Mozart, master of the ancient music magic. His instrument can enchant anyone to do his bidding, not to mention he can use it to increase the strength of those possessed, making them a quick ready-to-go army.'

Bob looked at him, another guardian here to kill them just his bloody luck.

'I said stop looking at him like that!' yelled Carly holding out her hands in the air. Her eyes began to glow a bright white, suddenly a swarm of bats came flying towards them screeching and hungry for blood.

'Look Out!' yelled Wolfe grabbing Bob and dragging him back into the room, shutting the door just as the Bats slam into it while some hit the window. Lucky Wolfe paid extra for reinforced glass, 'Carly can control any animal she wants, sometimes all of them, with that power on his side he has his own army!' A bat burst into the room through the window, 'God Damn, Con Artists!' he yelled using his talent to pick up the bed and threw it at the bat, smashing it back out the window and blocked the rest from getting it. Wolfe held it down so it doesn't budge from the rest of the bats impact.

'OK, all we gotta do is to stop that music, right?!' Bob yelled hammering some planks on the door, where does he get this stuff?

'It's not that simple for his music has a deadly curse,' he said moving to the centre of the room, Bob joining him so he can explain. 'Once the music plays, whoever hears, it will have their life force linked directly to it, if the music stops for any reason,

41

we will drop dead in a second,' he tensed up. He and Bob could still hear the music, he had faced powerful sorcerers before but none this powerful, 'I'm sorry Bob, but I'm afraid we are done for.'

Bob punched him in the face, Wolfe fell back a bit but stayed on his feet, wiping the blood from his nose as Bob ready his fist for another hit, 'Don't you give me that crap,' He punched him again this time in the cheek, 'You are the Taskmaster aren't you not? So stop whining like a little girl!' he said coldly.

'Well, do you have any ideas?' he said.

'The last two guardians have powerful magic but they both had weaknesses so we gotta figure out what his weakness is then kick his ass,' he replied looking at the door, 'So if you got time to give up and cry in the corner then you got time to think of a plan,' he took a step to the boarded up door. Wolfe stood beside him, Carly was depending on them to save her and to stop the guardian, so he will not let her down.

'It's quiet,' Bob said.

Wolfe nodded the smashing on the window and the door had stopped. The bats must have all knocked themselves out. 'Carly can summon any animal to her side as quickly as a fly flies into a window,' he told him, 'this isn't over, not by a long shot.'

In a second the door began banging much harder than a small bat, a loud roar filled the room along with more animal noises, howls of wolves, trumpets of an elephant, screeching of monkeys, baboons and the call of a gorilla just outside the door, the one that started the banging. Galloping noises slamming into the window and the walls came as well, there was a whole animal kingdom out there, waiting to come in.

'So all we gotta do is find the weakness,' said Wolfe cracking his neck, taking off his tie and chucking it on the bed, rolling up his sleeves for the fight is about to begin.

Bob nodded, cracking his fists together in his hands the two gentlemen prepared themselves just as a large hairy hand of an ape smashed a hole right through. 'You ever wrestled a gorilla before?' he asked him, Wolfe shook his head as he got into a fighting position. 'Well, you are going to do an old-fashioned Australian tradition,' Bob chuckled as he got into his own position.

The gorilla burst through the door, charging right at them with the music playing on full blast.

Chapter 5

The gorilla charged forward, smacking Bob to the wall and shoulder barged Wolfe right into the bathroom, Wolfe hitting his head on the toilet seat as he fell back from the gorilla, cursing under his breath, he watched the gorilla rip the door and hold it up like a shield, Slamming it down but Wolfe moved to the side and used his talent to pick up the bathtub, lifting it over his head, he threw it right in the ape's face.

The gorilla roared in pure rage, he used his huge palm to smack Wolfe across the face and knocked him back against the wall, then sending a furry fist straight at his head but he moved his head at the last moment, leaving it to go through the wall. The gorilla screeched more while Wolfe sent a few punches to his head, punching repeatedly with his talent to give him an advantage but the gorilla was a smart one and used his huge hand to try and smack him.

Wolfe ducked and moved to his other side, sending more beatings into its face, the gorilla fell limp on the ground, the attacks finally having an effect, he fell unconscious with his hand still in the wall.

Wolfe spat out blood, he limped out of the bathroom with one hand on the door. He caught Bob having trouble of his own as he got pummelled by two crocodiles on the bed, he had chains wrapped around his fists so his punches had much more effect to their heads, he then pulled out a hunting knife and quickly stabbed each one as many times as he could, but one got a lucky bite on his already injured shoulder, making him yell out in pain.

Wolfe charged forward with an intent to help him but the bear came out of nowhere and clawed his chest, making a huge claw mark across his shirt and cut deep within his skin making blood spill out. "Sweet Jeebus" the bear stabbed his abdomen with his other claw and lifted him up high, Wolfe sent strikes into its jaw, as well as a few charged up kicks into its neck. The bear roared and threw him across the room into the TV, static of electricity flashed and pieces of glass stab his shoulders, 'Oh I am so not getting a refund now.'

The bear roared so loud his eardrums burst, looking to the bed for a second he saw Bob using two hands to tear apart one of the crocodile's jaws, blood going everywhere on the bed and onto the other crocodile. The crocodile roared in memory of his brother, having the resolve to avenge him it clamped his jaws around Bob's leg, making him fall back. Wolfe did not have time to recover himself for the bear charged down at him, narrowly missing the taskmaster dodging forward and rolling under the bear, coming up to send a charged up punch into its back, the bear howled and Wolfe jumped high, kicking the huge animal into what's left of the TV, electrocuting it until it stopped moving.

The second crocodile fell from the bed, a large sword impaled its cranium it laid there not moving. Bob, huffing, got down from the bed, leg busted and bleeding and he could barely stand. He looked to Wolfe then they both turned to the door, now the bed had fallen from the destroyed window the wolves charged in, followed by the rest of the animals behind them they swarmed the two men.

'Where the hell are they coming from!' yelled Bob.

Where did the animals come from, you ask?

Few miles down the road, was the great nature zoo of awesome deadly animals! Here, people could have a tour of the zoo facilities, seeing the prized bloody gorilla, who was known for his ruthless beating of innocent bystanders, but what he hated most of all is bald people.

Or the great wolves of night hunt, they said that these wolves' blood thirst and power exceeded normal limits at night, no one would want to find yourself getting hunted by these beasts late in the night.

But the zoo's greatest treasure was the godlike bear, a huge oversized monster who was always accompanied by his two crocodile minions; they ganged up on one prey and left the remains for the bear to continue ripping and mauling to its death, also a penalty of fifty grand if anything, like killing the bear, happened to this majestic creature.

Now, the events began on one simple night, a night guard named Randy was in the bathroom after he ate that taco for dinner which was two weeks old that he bought last month in a takeaway shop. He left it in the staff fridge and never touched it until tonight when he was so hungry, he took it out and ate it, regretted it immediately afterwards, he ran to the toilets leaving the animals free to unlock their cages.

Man, never leaving food in the fridge again, he said to himself walking out, stopping short at all the cages of their killer animals, they really needed to change that sign on top that says "Killer Animals", all open and empty inside. Knowing he will get blamed for this, he did the responsible thing, taking out his phone and dialling up his manager, 'Um, sir, all the cages are open and the animals are gone.'

'WHAT?! HOW COULD THIS HAPPEN, I GAVE YOU ONE JOB TO KEEP THE FISHES DRY AND YOU CAN'T EVEN DO THAT?!' his voiced boomed from the speaker, forcing his rage on the poor night guard.

Randy pulled back from the phone, 'But you told me to watch the zoo…'

'WHAT? WHO IS THIS?!'

'Randy?'

'RANDELL?'

'No, he's the fisher man.'

'AH YES! MAN, HE WAS A GREAT POKER BUDDY, SO WHO IS THIS?'

'Randy…'

'Rindy?'

'Randy.'

'Candy?'

'RANDY.'

'Michael?'

'Ran, where did you get Michael?'

'RANDY THE USELESS TOILET GUY?! HOW THE HELL DID THE ANIMALS GET OUT?!'

'Well, if you did not put the locks on the inside…' Randy tried to explain but the manager yelled more, not even in English now just spouting all angry gibberish with colourful words and different curse words in different languages.

'You know what boss, I'm going on a break,' Randy said then hung up, chucking the phone away, he walked casually out of the zoo.

Wolfe charged his fists at the wolves pouncing on top him, knocking them to his sides while Bob shot the rest with a Tommie gun, but that won't last long as more relentless animals came into the room looking for more chaos, 'We are not gonna last long!' yelled Bob.

Wolfe nodded, running forward, he charged into Bob, grabbing his blood-stained jumpsuit and barged the wall, sending them both crashing into the next room where a young couple, newly wedded from the way they were underdressed, screamed from the top of their bed trying to cover themselves.

Wolfe covered his eyes, his face going red, 'So sorry for this intrusion, but you need to leave, right now!' he told them turning his face away so he could open his eyes, seeing Bob getting to his feet and ignoring the almost naked couple.

The music played louder now, the newlyweds could hear it coming from the window. The girl got out from the bed and walked towards it. 'Such beautiful music…' she said entranced

'No, you must not listen!' yelled Wolfe.

It was too late, the girl figure began morphing, her shoulder getting broader her legs grew higher, nails turning into sharp claws while her jaw grew stronger teeth, powerful enough to tear off bone and flesh along with a hunchback. With saliva running down her new jaw line, she turned to the two fighters with a lust for their blood.

Her partner joined in the transformation; growing big hands himself the hunches upward, his legs now fast enough to outrun a cheetah. 'Hey Babe, let's see how many bones we can eat from these two,' he said in a possessed monster voice, looking to his wife who prepared herself to pounce.

'So, I take the guy, you take the girl,' said Bob wiping blood off his head.

Wolfe was about to say a rather colourful word but the girl already pounced on him, sending him onto his back, Wolfe moved his head so her jaws did not bite it clean off. Her claws digging into his already bloody chest making him scream, using all his strength he threw a kick to her side and knocked her off. Meanwhile, Bob was holding the guy by his tail, because of course he had a tail now, and spun him around like bowser from Super Mario, sending him into his wife, and they collided and fell into the bathroom, Wolfe closing the door behind them and used his talent to charge up the door so it could hold them, so it could be as strong as a titanium wall.

Bob came up behind him, 'You can charge up stuff too?' he asked.

Wolfe nodded, 'Yeah, I can make them stronger than any normal item,' he said.

'Then why the hell did you not use it on our door or window?!' he asked in a very ticked off tone.

Wolfe was about to answer, but did not say anything 'cause he really did have a point.

'Well, if you can charge up normal items then I got an idea, how loud can you make a speaker?'

'Ear-popping loud, you're planning to drown out the music, aren't you?' he asked.

'Yeah, will it work? If everyone only hears our music on top of his, it won't matter if his instrument breaks, right?'

'I don't know,' he only said, 'We don't know the extent of his magic.'

'Well, we are going to die anyway, so why not take the risk,' Bob told him.

Wolfe nodded, the two men went to the door and kicked it open to the carpark filled with more animals and mutated motel guests. Some were standing on the cars while others were on the rooftops waiting for the command to kill.

'Looks like hell comes knocking,' said Wolfe.

They spot Carly sitting in a meditation position on top of the van, her eyes glowing full red and keeping her control on the animals while Mozart stood behind her playing his clarinet louder for all the mutated guests to become stronger.

'Ah, the mice found themselves out of the frying pan and into the stove,' the guardian said putting his clarinet in the air while it still played the deadly music.

'That's not how that metaphor works!' yelled Bob.

'Ah, but I know all the metaphors,' Mozart bowed, then he began to say more metaphors and sayings that did not make any sort of sense that Wolfe and Bob felt embarrassed just by looking at him.

'I'll get to the radio and turn my music up, you distract the army of killer animals and people,' he told Bob casually sneaking around them.

'Sure leave me with the hard stuff,' he mumbled to himself beginning his charge into them, he jumped up and started running on their heads like a crowd at a disco soon getting to the van where Carly sat, kicking her in her ribs so she could fall to ground and lose her control over the animals, that's one problem down. The animals soon got back into their senses; with no one pulling their strings they began attacking the mutated motel guests.

And that's another problem solved, Wolfe thought to himself running and dodging each and every person or animal until he reached the van. He grabbed the handle just as Bob was sent flying over his head and knocked into the transformed manager who was knocked back into another killer bear, which was now mauling both of them. Mozart looked down upon Wolfe entering the van and locking the door behind him, 'My Sweet Flower, kill him for me, will you?' he asked of her holding a rose in his hand for her to claim.

The rose was all she needed to get on her feet and charged at the door. Wolfe started the car, and tuned the radio on a catchy tune. 'Come on,' he said soon picking one by Bruno Mars, placing his palm on it he soon began to charge up the volume so it will block the music completely from everyone's ears before Mozart stops it, but then suddenly Carly's hand burst through the glass and wrapped her arm around his throat, pulling him back and preventing him from charging the radio, his free hand under her arm while the other reached desperately for it. By putting her hand through the window she had glass shards imbedding into her hand and arm, making them even more lethal for they had reached Wolfe's throat and started digging in, if her arm went any deeper he would choke on his own blood.

He needed all his talent for the radio which meant he couldn't just use it to push her arm back, the music was already loud but not loud enough. Carly was too far gone to snap out of it, so she had begun pulling back making the shards go deeper. Wolfe was doing all he could to push back and reach for the radio but it felt like she had also been given incredible strength.

'Give up,' Mozart said to him standing behind Carly, 'You know my music has also mutated dear Carly as well, so you can see this has been a pointless waste of effort,' he smiled that conniving smile of his, 'A wise man will know he is beaten and you, sir, are beaten.'

Bob was too busy punching the mutated manager and kicking the killer bear, who both decided to gang up on him. He won't be able to reach Wolfe in time. Knowing it is all down to him, Wolfe grunted and pulled forward, he was a taskmaster and he will not die like this. Her arm dug even deeper so it had drawn blood now, any deeper and he would choke. Carly was doing everything she could to stop him, even started using her free hand to punch him in the back of the head. This sudden attack struck him cold that his vision had started going black.

Mozart gave a cheery laugh, 'You are strong my good sir, I'll give you that,' he clasped his Clarinet, 'I have enjoyed this night I tell you, met a pretty girl that I will be sorry to kill but it's time for the song to end.'

The music stopped.

Roaring with all of his might Wolfe pushed forward and slammed his palm on the radio making the music burst out of the speakers! Bruno Mars blasting into the ears of everyone in the town making the lights open in houses and buildings along the streets, sirens blazing and windows smashing, dogs barking at the sudden burst of strange noise. Carly let go of him so she could cover her ears from the loud noise, along with the mutated guests and animals running away into all directions. But it was Mozart who got the full force of it, clasping his ears he screamed in high pitch while his ears bled.

Wolfe gasped for air and held his neck in place, managing to avoid his throat being slit open. 'It's over,' he said sitting back; Wolfe's talent had burnt up the radio to the point that it caught on fire. But it had blocked out the guardian's music just before it had killed everyone.

Mozart sobbed and screamed, he removed his hands so he could try to hear anything. He listened to the sounds of animals running around and the confused people in ripped clothing that had reverted back and getting scared and confused of what happened. But he could not hear one single tear drop from them at all. 'NO! You have deafened my wonderful ears! I cannot hear the sweet sounds of my music ever again!' he wallowed, 'The greatest musician, unable to hear the music he plays!' he looked at Wolfe gasping in the front seat of the van, looking at him in his eyes. Wolfe looked back and uttered a curse word. 'I may not hear but my music can still kill everyone!' he said looking around for his Clarinet, he saw the radio on fire so he knew that his damn song had stopped, giving him the chance to kill them all at once.

'Looking for this?' Bob said behind him, holding his clarinet in his hand, but Mozart did not seem to hear him while he got to the ground searching desperately for his clarinet, 'Hey! Can you hear me?' Bob called out to him, but he did not get a reply. Sighing, he snapped the clarinet on his knee and chucked one half over his head.

The half flew past his eyes, Mozart screamed at the broken part he turned just in time to see Bob smash the other part under his boot. Mozart screamed like a wounded animal, jumping off his knees he tried to pick up the pieces hoping to put it all back together or at least make music out of it. 'I have to make sweet music,' he said not hearing his own words, he looked up at Bob and backed away so fast he tried getting up on his feet but not before seeing another person standing behind him, the figure of the girl looking very angry at him.

'My sweet flower, lend me the strength of your courage and finish them off for me?' he asked her hoping in that sweet calming accent of his. If he could still use her, then she could kill those two for him then he will kill her.

But without his music she was immune to him, more so due to not liking being used and manipulated like that. She looked down at him with such rage in her eyes she threw a right hook into his face and broke his nose. He burst out blood and fell backwards, grabbing his nose to stop the bleeding. 'I gotta get out of here!' he cried turning around and crawling desperately away from her but Bob quickly grabbed his hair, stopping him in his tracks and pulling him back so he is held up to face him. Mozart turned to face him, 'Oh, the prisoner, you're not still mad about this whole scenario, right? I wasn't even going to kill you just these two, you understand right?'

Bob held his hair tighter, his eyes blazing with such hatred, 'Please don't punch me, the girl already broke my nose what

51

more can you do to me?' he begged, Bob mumbled something to him but he could not hear, in his fear he assumed he was going to let him go, 'Oh, thank you! Thank you, you are so kind, I promise I will never hunt you ever again,' Bob smiled and shook his head. Mozart held his breath, he opened his mouth to say something that will save him but Bob struck a fist into his face.

Bob roared and punched him into the windscreen of the car, injuring his back with glass shards he was thrown through it, out cold in a heartbeat.

The guardian was down, Bob left him to rot on some bloke's car but Carly had other ideas. She lit up her eyes with the same red glow and the pack of wolves came back, growling and snarling at the guardian getting ready to maul him. She was about to send out the command when Bob grabbed her arm and pulled her back. 'Stop,' he said coldly to her.

Carly blinked back her eyes to normal. 'Why should I? He was going to kill us and everyone here, he needs to die otherwise he will do it again,' she said pushing herself away from him. Bob just glared at her. Carly shivered with rage, her heart pounding under her ribcage. 'Just turn around if it's too much for you,' she said, but he did not say a word. The wolves shook off their control and ran off before something else happens to them.

Wolfe stepped out of the van holding his neck. 'We should leave before the authorities arrive, also I think I might be dying,' he said calmly falling forwards, Bob catching him in his arm.

'Carly go find us a new ride, I'm going to patch this prick up so we can leave,' he told her forcing Wolfe into the back of the van.

Carly looked to the guardian and back, taking a deep breath she turned and went to find an open car that was easy to steal and not destroyed by mutants. Wolfe laid back watching Bob grab a needle and flicking the top. 'This will null the pain,' he said sticking it in his neck, Wolfe cried out from the sudden prick. 'Also, it will be painful first, should've mentioned that,' he chuckled.

'Eh, it's not like I've been stabbed in the neck or anything,' he mumbled.

Bob grabbed a needle and a thread and began stitching up his neck, closing the wounds as best as he could but he needed to get him to a hospital.

'No, take me to the hub, they will take care of it,' Wolfe told him.

'Can your people fix this wound?' he asked.

'Don't worry, we have the best medicine out there,' Wolfe assured him, 'Thank you for stopping her,' he added looking out to Carly.

Bob cut the thread and chucked the needle away. He turned his head to her as well, 'Your student has problems mate, you do know that, right?'

'It's the world we live in, she has seen a lot of things you never got to see,' he sighed, 'Like what?'

Wolfe was about to answer, but he soon got distracted by birds singing the rhyme of Disney to him, flying around his head with those big anime eyes of theirs. 'Oh, it seems the birds have come to take me away,' he said softly closing his eyes.

Bob gave himself a face palm, great the morphine kicked in.

Carly found them the car that belonged to the newlyweds, not like they will miss it. They took it and sped off into the night, Wolfe sprayed out in the back while Carly sat in the front seat, and Bob driving them before the cops showed up a split second later.

'Oh, I could feel the cold hands of death touching my chest,' Wolfe bellowed out reaching out in the air, 'Oh my, is that Jesus? No, it's Marty Mcfly, I did not know you were dead how have you been?' Bob and Carly looked at each other with raised eyebrows listening to his nonsense ramblings.

'This is gonna be a long night,' groaned Bob.

Carly nodded, taking the last shard out of her bloody arm and throwing it out the window. She then rested her head on her arm and watched the rising sun. Bob looked at her from the side, watching her blank cold stare. 'If you're trying to mimic me it's not funny,' he said to her hoping to get a comeback, but she did not give one.

'Oh, there you are Gooey the Pink Elephant, please, help me from this fatal mortal coil of mine.'

'I could not let you take a life,' Bob finally said to her.

'You have no right,' mumbled Carly, doing her best to avoid looking at him.

'Oh of course, I understand, you are a busy elephant and all with your many appearances in television.'

'I know he killed a lot of people before us, I know the kind of guy he is,' he said looking at her still ignoring everything he is saying. Bob groaned, 'Hey!' he yelled making her jump, 'What you feel right now is nothing compared to what will happen if you killed him, it will eat you alive and keep you awake,' Carly continued to ignore him. Bob tightened his fingers around the steering wheel, starting to lose his temper he slammed the brake, making her fall into the dashboard and Wolfe falling to the ground.

'Jesus, why did you stop the party bus? I was about to get my groove on.'

'What the hell?' Carly yelled out to him but Bob already got out of the car. They were parked on the side of the road deep in the outback. Her door flew open and Bob came to drag her out by her arm, throwing her to the ground, 'What's the big idea?' she yelled at him getting to her feet.

'You wanna kill someone?' Bob said to her holding up his hands, 'Then kill me.'

Chapter 6

Mickle stood on top of a rock, observing the great Ayres Rock of Australia. The dawn breaking over the horizon on his silhouette, for he had been observing and learning, soon coming up with a way to break inside.

These humans sure know how to keep magic out, he said to himself, he spent one hour looking at all the different kind of symbols etched into the walls, ancient ones to keep sorcerers and guardians out unless they had permission to enter, like say, getting escorted in by a taskmaster. The top only opened to flying crafts, and sometimes the pizza plane which he never knew existed.

He took a knee; to get in he had to be conniving, tactical as it were, looking down at some soldiers driving around in a buggy on their regular patrol around the garden areas. Seeing his chance, he stepped off the rock, floating in the air, he made a soft landing on the ground, running towards them at break neck speed. He sprinted across the desert, jumped over some wildlife, he charged over the car and stopped just between the six men all standing around him.

The garden was out of sight of the base, making this simple for Mickle to begin his tactic. One soldier pulled out his gun but Mickle grabbed it, crushing the barrel with his fingers and jabbed one finger into his throat, making a hole for the blood to come pouring out.

Now the rest began firing, bullets pierced his body but Mickle could not be harmed for mortal weapons had no effect on him, he spread out his arm and stood back, making one big leap between the men behind him and immediately decapitated their heads, sending them rolling in the air and land on the ground afar.

Three men left, one ran to his car for his phone but Mickle took one leg and held it up, his other pushing from the ground to send a bullet speed kick into his back. His foot broke through his belly, bone and organ blew out from the impact of his kick making him scream in terror and fall to ground with no more air to breathe. Mickle took his foot out of his back and kicked the blood off.

He turned to the last two. *What will they do?* he wondered. Charged at him with guns blazing or run away like small children. The two men screamed and charged at him, guns blazing they ran past him and towards the rock. A little bit of both he guessed.

He bounced off the ground by his toes and leaped backwards, using his hands, he grabbed a hold of their heads and held himself upside down over them, giving them a smile, he smashed them together like two pumpkins exploding on impact with one another. He stood back down on the remains and began his next phase of the plan, stripping them out of their clothing.

He put on the shirt, pants, belt and any other thing that made a soldier fitted on, he put the cap on so to cover his eyes and tied his hair back. Now that he had disguised himself, he could just walk right into their base, and no one will ever be the wiser. Walking for hours to the rock, he stood by the big empty wall where he watched soldiers come back and forth from a huge garage door that opened up. Knocking on the wall a hatch opened to the side for a face to look through. 'State your name,' he said.

Crap, he did not bother asking for a name from the dead soldiers. 'Commander Elkcim,' replied Mickle hiding his hands behind his back, he really got to remember to wash the blood off after he kills.

'Never heard of you.'

'Its Spanish, for not a sorcerer,' continued Mickle.

'Oh, well, in that case come right in,' the guard said proudly. 'You'll be surprised how many we got here,' he pushed a button for the huge garage door to open up next to the hatch, opening it to the huge headquarters hidden inside.

Mickle thanked the man as he strolled in, chuckling quietly at how dumb these mortals were. Now to find the key to release his brother from his prison, after all it will be easy to find it. All he had to do was go to the main building and look around for the item in question, the item that is the key that is not supposed to be a key but he will find it.

Mickle proceeded to the bathroom to bang his head against the wall. He had no idea what the damn key looked like.

'Are you serious?' Carly said to him.

Bob stood, not moving or talking he waited for her to strike first, Carly was not going to bother talking to him so she decided to punch him in his smug face, just to show him that she was not someone to play around with, but Bob grabbed her fist in mid-air and twisted it, sending a jab at her belly. Carly yelled in pain and fell to her knees, Bob still holding her hand tight.

'What's the matter? I thought you said you're someone I wouldn't want to mess with,' he said letting go of her hand.

Carly gave a small growl and did a sweeping kick to his feet, but Bob used his boot to stomp on her ankle sending a sharp pain up her leg. 'Killing that guardian will not make you feel better, that is a road a girl of your age shouldn't go down even if you are a taskmaster in training,' he said.

Carly got to her feet and charged at him with a fist raised, she tried to punch his stupid face but he dodged and elbowed her chin. Unable to handle it anymore, Carly lit up her eyes to summon an animal to help her but he just used two fingers to poke her in the eyes.

Carly blinked back tears, rubbing her sore eyes from the pain. 'You are powerful, I'll give you that, hell, I just saw it first-hand but your eyes are your only weakness, you can't use your talent if your eyes get damaged,' Bob said, watching her rub her eyes in pain, 'If you finish fighting then start talking, tell me what your problem is.'

Carly then started to blindly throw punches, hoping to at least hit him but Bob just held her head, holding her back with no effort while she failed miserably trying to hit him. Bob sighed to himself, 'Look Wolfe is bleeding out and I don't know how long he has...'

'Oh my, the tavern is so furry, is that you Freddy? Have you come to take me to dreamland?' mumbled Wolfe from the floor of the car.

Bob pushed her back, 'If you don't want to talk about your problem then it's fine by me, but if we are going to work together we need to start getting along, I know you don't trust me and I

57

don't care,' he walked to the driver's side taking one last look at her, 'Look it's just like Wolfe said, you're stuck with me as I am stuck with you,' he got back into the driver's seat, waiting for her to get in before starting the car. Carly took a deep breath and got back in the car as well.

They drove in silence until the sun reached the sky, Carly took a glance at Bob with his eyes on the road. She sighed to herself, her heart heavy as she whispered, 'The guardians killed my family.'

Bob's eyes looked at her; she just ignored him and continued to stare out the window. She did not need his pity, not from him of all people since he did not understand the real side of this world, what prices she paid for living in it. Bob turned back to the road and let the silence eat the air away, lucky they still got Wolfe's hallucinations to listen to.

'Oh Freddy, your hands are so smooth…'

Bob sent his hand back and knocked him out cold. 'Yeah, we don't want to hear anything more,' he said putting his hand back on the wheel, Wolfe knocked out on the ground.

Carly continued to look out at the barren outback thinking about what Bob said. How could he know what she's going through, since he never killed that guardian that killed his friend, nor did he kill that guardian back at the parking lot. In fact, she suspected he did not kill the guardian back at the café. *Has he ever killed anyone?* She took a quick glance at him; how can he walk in this dark side of the world without taking a single life?

He was covered with blood from head to toe, his jumpsuit ripped, skin scratched and bitten, yet he still saved her life time and time again without any thought. Great now she felt guilty for fighting with him, she groaned in her head, turning away. 'Thank you,' she said softly so he doesn't hear.

But he smirked, *What a jackass.*

Hours passed, Carly fell asleep with her head on the window feeling the rumbling of the road underneath the wheels; it was comforting in a way until Bob yelled out, 'CAR!' and stepped on the brakes hard, sending her forward and grabbing the dashboard quickly.

Carly screamed and held on bracing for impact but Bob just chuckled to himself and drove the car casually. 'What the actual hell, man?' she yelled at him.

'Consider that payback for that animal attack back at the motel.'

'I wasn't in control last night!' she argued sitting back.

Bob just chuckled and stopped the car, 'Glad to see your attitude is OK, also I think we're here,' he turned back to the backseat and slapped Wolfe's face, 'Wake up you old geezer, is this the place?' he pointed out the window. Wolfe mumbled and sat up the best he could.

Carly looked out, stepping out of the car to see the huge rock in the middle of the outback, Ayres Rock was what it's called, the great big red rock of Australia. Wolfe said they needed to come here but she could not see any sign of a building, tent or even a tunnel. Granted, she had never been to this headquarters before.

Wolfe got himself back on the seat, 'Yeah that's the place, now hurry you need to get to the...' he trailed off then fell back onto the seat, knowing time was short, Bob, started the car just as Carly quickly sat back in.

'This is bad, he needs a doctor now,' he said speeding down towards the huge rock.

Carly looked back at Wolfe who was starting to go pale, 'Faster, we can't let him die like this,' she said.

'Well, how did you picture him dying?' replied Bob.

'Well, I always imagined him fighting dragon bears... HEY that's not the point right now!' she yelled actually getting worried, Bob was driving the car at breakneck speed, trying to find some sort of entrance but there was nothing but rock. 'Dammit old man,' he sighed, 'I can't find a way to get in, you sure this is the right rock?'

'It has to be,' Carly said.

Bob stopped the car after the second time around. 'Now what?' he said slamming his hand on the wheel.

Carly shook her head. 'I don't know,' she just said.

Bob grunted, banging his fists on the wheel now while he yelled out the same cursed word over. Tears started to drop from Carly's eyes; she had no idea how to save her mentor now. The nearest town was 18 miles ahead. They'll never make it on time. Then suddenly a hatch opened up just in front of them. Both Bob and Carly stared at the small hatch showing the eyes of a person, 'What is your business here?' he asked calmly.

Carly got out of the car; while Bob got the engine ready just in case this was another trap, 'I'm Carly Blake, I'm the apprentice of Taskmaster Wolfe,' she began.

'Ah yes, Wolfe told us all about you,' his eyes beamed if that's a thing, 'How is that imaginary pony of yours? What was his name again?'

'Butters is real! I mean…' she blushed, 'Wolfe is dying and we need medical attention right away,' she pointed to the car.

The guard nodded. 'Sure, just come right in,' he said as he pushed a button to open the huge garage door that is perfectly camouflaged just from the side, allowing them to enter. Bob started the car to drive in, Carly walking back but then the soldiers came running out, one of them grabbing Carly and dragging her inside. Bob's eyes widened, they all ran towards him and formed around the car, pointing their guns right at his head, if this was a joke then Bob wasn't laughing.

'PUT THEM UP!' yelled the closest soldier, jabbing the rifle into his face. Bob glared as he slowly put his hands up, 'Make any sudden moves and you'll get a couple in the head.'

More soldiers came to the back, opening it to pull Wolfe out and getting him on a stretcher, so they could bring him inside safely, medical doctors and nurses rushing to care for his wounds. Carly head butted the soldier holding her and ran back out to stop them. 'Stop, what are you doing he's with us!' she yelled standing at the car and pushing the soldier away.

Another soldier grabbed her and hauled her back inside while another soldier opened the door and dragged Bob out. 'Stand down!' he yelled putting the barrel to his head making sure Bob stayed on his knees, looking pretty pissed at this point for he did not expect getting his head blown off. Carly struggled in the soldier's grip, then she spotted someone walking out of the base right past her, she managed to get out so she could watch the commander walking up to the prisoner.

He was a broad gentlemen, army uniform neat and ironed with his black hair polished and clean cut, he stood over Bob and introduced himself, 'Greetings, I am Commander Jim Harrison, these are my soldiers that have their guns on you,' Bob just glared up at him like he broke his glass of beer. 'We have been expecting you, Mr Stewart,' he finished.

Carly forced herself back to them. 'Listen, he's with us so don't hurt him,' she pleaded.

'You are seriously injured, Wolfe is bleeding out, this gentleman is wearing a prison uniform and covered in blood,' he pointed out, Carly cursed to herself, she knew that that outfit will get him in trouble, 'As protocol we must have him contained and interrogated.'

'He has beaten three guardians,' Carly argued, hoping that'll get him off the hook at least.

Jim nodded, 'Yes and from our reports killed one as well,' Carly quickly looked at Bob, the shock on her face while he continued, 'Drybon was found dead yesterday evening, a charred corpse with no eyes found in an alleyway, few blocks from the crime scene.'

'I did not kill him,' said Bob.

'Does not matter, what matters is that you are a dangerous man, we have to determine if you will be a threat to our organisation,' Jim waved his finger for another soldier to grab Carly, dragging her back inside, 'Send her to the med bay for treatment,' he told him, 'And use your talent to hold her if you have to.'

Carly struggled out of his grip but she soon stopped, looking at Bob raising his hand to give the signal that he'll be OK alone. Carly sighed, she stopped struggling and allowed to be led inside.

She marvelled at how big the place was, different dome buildings for different things assembled around a cul de sac road, forming a tiny town. There were street lamps, parks and schools along with cafes, hospitals, research centres and training grounds, all standing around the huge dome building in the middle of the oval road forming the main hub where the boss of this sector resides, along with the rest of the taskmasters getting their objectives, missions and holiday pays.

Carly was taken to the hospital, where they walked into crowds of soldiers who were injured, wounded or some missing a leg or an entire torso according to that one guy over there. Carly was signed in at the reception and taken to a private room to be treated; she was sitting on the bed and waited for the doctor to walk in.

Her doctor's name was Margaret, a respectable doctor for she was the best in the field, with that sassy attitude as well as her skills. 'How the hell did you get glass into your arm?' she asked her grabbing her arms to inspect the damage, picking up some pliers to take the tiny pieces still left in her bare flesh.

Carly winced. 'There was a battle,' she began.

'Hmm hmmm,' she hummed, 'There is always a battle with you apprentices,' she continued taking the glass out, Carly feeling the pain from her arm as she started bleeding again, 'You young ones are always looking for adventures, not caring that it will be your last.'

Once Margaret was done, she lifted up her shirt to examine her injuries. 'Dear god, what happened? You got multiple punches to your abdomen, broken ribs and a scarring on your head,' she said hitting the wound on her head with a pen.

'Well, the head was from that guardian,' said Carly rubbing her sore head from the pen.

'Oh, I see, and where did you get the rest?'

Carly hesitated, the rest was from Bob kicking her multiple times. Margaret sighed, she had begun bandaging her forehead. 'Shirt off,' she said bandaging her ribs after she took her shirt off.

While she was getting bandaged Carly decided to ask, 'So where is Wolfe?'

'He is in surgery, don't worry the injuries on his neck and chest are taken care of, although, it wasn't helped by that horrible stitching he received,' she said. 'Give it a few days, your mentor will be on his feet in no time,' she finished wrapping her belly in a bandaged, now starting to disinfect the open wounds on her arm, the liquid burning like hell but Carly got through it, after all she had a lot on her mind at the moment.

It's good that Wolfe was going to be fine, he was stronger than anyone she knew, but she could not get over the fact that Bob killed one of the guardians, After all that he said about not killing, true she wasn't conscious at that time, so she did not know the full story only what Bob told her.

Seeing her blank stare, Margaret tapped her forehead yet again to send a sharp pain through her skull, she finished disinfecting and bandaging her arm. 'You're thinking about that prisoner, aren't you?' she said.

Carly looked at her. 'How do you know about him?' she asked.

'My talent of course, I can know anything that goes on in my workplace,' she said.

'That sounds invasive.'

'Great for gossip,' she said putting her head back up, 'For example my nurse is doing it with doctor Steve down the hall right now.'

Carly gave a small giggle. 'What are they going to do to him?' she asked, unable to believe she was actually worried about him, of all people.

'Well, honey, if he doesn't pass the Commander's test, then he'll be in worse shape than you.'

Mickle stepped out of the bathroom, after hours of banging his head, he came to the conclusion that he needed someone to lead him to the key. Lucky no one came in during that time which was bizarre even for him. Then he spotted the sign that said "quarantine" for there was deadly insects that took control of the bathrooms. Mickle slowly backed away.

Walking out, he saw the taskmaster Wolfe being pushed on a carrier towards the hospital, guess Mozart failed in killing him, at least he damaged the pathetic human to near death so that was something. But he saw this as an opportunity for Wolfe could lead him to the key, then he will kill him quickly.

He followed them to the hospital, coming up with his majestic plan to be an ordinary soldier body guarding them until they discover the location of the key.

Then he will solve all his problems in one day.

Chapter 7

'Well, Davey what do we have?' officer Liam asked the young officer at the desk.

The station is quiet today, some reports coming in that weren't too serious, hell the only important thing was the suspect they had in a holding cell, crying and moaning over his broken instrument. Davey the young officer in training stood up, 'Well, sir, our suspect isn't saying anything, actually he is talking but not answering our question since he is too busy crying about his clarinet.'

'Figures.'

'We got the report from the witnesses, they all say he was their master and he made them all into monsters and controlling all the animals from the zoo.'

'The same animals from the zoo down the street?'

'The very one sir.'

'Good god,' he sighed walking down the hallway, Davey walking beside him, 'Let me handle this guy, the toughest brick can be settled with a little water.'

'Pardon.'

'Just a metaphor that I made up.'

'I don't think you should make up metaphors...'

'Oh, shut it we're here,' Liam said walking into the holding cells, there was the perp right there, sobbing and cradling his broken clarinet. His face covered in blood and bruises making him look like a pounded meatloaf.

Liam stood in front of his cell. 'Quit your crying already!' he yelled to him.

'My beautiful darling clarinet...' Sobbed Mozart.

He banged the cell, 'I said quit your crying! We got questions for you to answer!' the perp turned his head towards them, dropping his broken instrument, 'Better, now you are going to explain what you did at the sleazy Motel last night…'

'Oh brother! You're here in my dying hour of need!' Mozart called out getting to his feet.

Liam and Davey frowned, turning around they saw a tall gentleman behind them wearing black sunglasses staring at them. 'Move now,' he told them.

Liam pointed a finger at him, 'Listen mate, you have no clearance to be in here so get lost before I drag your sorry ass out!'

The gentleman held up his hand, extending one finger he poked the officer right through the head. The body fell to the ground just as Davey pulled out his gun, but he never got to use it because the gentlemen's finger slid across the air, sending a ripple of wind through his neck. Davey stood still, he could feel his head slowly slipping off his shoulders and fall to the ground, rolling away while he watched his body fall along with him.

Mozart came close to the bars, 'Thank you, my dear brother, now get me out of here, so I may continue my hunt for the Taskmaster and the apprentice.'

'You got beaten by them,' Mr Red said silently.

'A minor setback, I assure you.'

'Yet, I can't trust you to do your job,' Mr Red took off his glasses, 'Our Brother is locked up and with no way to return, so it is our duty to free him but we can't do that with you getting beaten by mortals,' he looked directly into his eyes.

Mozart gasped, looking into the eyes he stood back, 'Brother please, give me one more chance!' he fell to his knees, smoke coming out of his pupils. 'Do not judge me, please!' he begged looking up at him.

Mr Red stared directly at him, not looking away while he began to burn, soon his skin charred and was cracked black. He fell to the ground with a loud thud, his eyes burning craters right now.

He put his glasses back on; looking to the two dead mortals he waved his right hand so they could be absorbed into the ground, melting into it you could say so the two dead bodies became smooth and flat. 'These mortals are starting to annoy me,' he said walking out.

He left the police station behind, walking along the sandy highway of the outback, 'Mickle should have no problem finding the key; he is the third powerful out of the rest of us,' he stopped, looking up at the sky, 'Still if this continues, then I might have to dirty my own hands with their filthy mortal blood.'

He continued walking along the highway, a man with a mission and a purpose.

Chapter 8

Commander Jim was a patient man, he liked to do his job and service to his country.

Standing behind the one-way mirror, he watched his latest objective through the window, the prisoner named Robert Stewart, or Bob as he preferred to be called. He had him handcuffed to the table but that did not stop him from sitting casually in his chair, leaning back while he waited for the Commander to enter just so he could get this over with.

Jim walked into the room, holding a mug of coffee for him and placed it on the table. 'Coffee,' he said coldly, not a question just pointing it out.

'You're doing it wrong,' Bob just said.

'I beg your pardon,' Jim replied kindly sitting on the table casually himself but making glaring faces at him.

'The good cop, bad cop routine, you are doing a mixture of them,' he said glaring back, refused to be intimidated by some old geezer, he would rather have Wolfe back.

Now he was caught Jim stood up tall. 'Well, you seem like a tough dude,' he said shining the light in his face. 'So tell me "Bob", he said that name like he was spitting something nasty out, 'Where did all that blood come from?'

'From me, where else could it come from,' replied Bob, showing him the soaked bandages and claw marks, along with teeth marks in his shoulder which were still bleeding.

Jim had a strong stomach so he will not be intimidated by the sight of blood or bones sticking out of places, which is why he did not just walk out of the room, headed into the nearest bathroom and proceeded to puke his breakfast into the toilet.

He came back dabbing his chin with his handkerchief. 'I see,' he said holding back a bit of his brunch, if Bob had a sense of humour, he would be laughing his head off right now. He sat back in his seat, 'Now next question, why are you here.'

'To find the key to the first guardians' prison so the other guardians don't get it and kill us all,' he said.

Jim nodded. 'Yes, I'm told you took down three guardians already, one three years ago that resulted in your imprisonment, and two yesterday,' he concluded.

'Yeah, it was a busy day.'

'Listen up "Bob"' Jim said slamming his hand on the table, 'The people here are under protection by me, if you plan on hurting them or destroying this base then we are gonna be new best friends,' he threatened.

Bob leaned forward. 'This isn't exactly on my bucket list mate, I just want to get the guardians off my back so if helping Wolfe in his mission does that, then anyone that gets in my way is going to lose,' he threatened him as well, so he knew exactly what he's capable of.

Jim glared at him, 'Very well, let's take a walk.'

Carly took ages finding the room Wolfe was in, having a new jacket to cover her bandages she knocked on every random door, seeing some weird never to be mentioned or "described" stuff. So don't even ask. However, one door involved a penguin washing his lipstick and looking like a bear.

Peeking in the thirteenth door, she sighed in relief at Wolfe, resting on the bed. He spotted her and gestured her to come in. 'There you are, got worried Bob had beaten you senseless,' he chuckled.

'Hey, I thought you were out of it,' she said walking in and sitting on the chair.

'Not that out of it, did it help?' he asked.

Carly looked down. 'Sorta, I can't stop thinking about what he said,' she admitted, 'All my life I dreamt about ending the guardians, I had my one chance last night but he took it from me.'

'You mean stopped you from making a mistake,' Wolfe corrected her.

Carly looked up at him. 'Do you think he's right, I mean he did kill that guardian that attacked us at the café,' she told him trying to find some reason not to listen.

'And who told you that?'

'The commander…' Carly trailed off, feeling really stupid right then.

'Commander Jim, you do remember he claimed a duck car jacked him and rode off to Vegas in Australia, right?' He chuckled.

'Well, when you say it like that…'

'So, you also remember that he dragged our unconscious bodies into that ambulance van and left right?' he reminded her making her feel more stupid. 'Don't worry you were probably still pissed at him for some reason or the other,' he said.

'Still am,' she mumbled.

'Speaking of which, what happened to him?' he finally asked.

'He was hauled off with Commander Jim, they're going to test him to see if he is a threat to the base,' explained Carly.

Wolfe sighed, 'Great, Commander Jim is someone you don't want to piss off, so we better hope Bob can walk out as a free man, or in a body bag.'

'Is he really that bad?' Carly asked

Wolfe chuckled, 'I've known Jim a long time, if he distrusts someone, be sure he will do whatever it takes to expose them for who they are, but if we're lucky he can see that our "friend" is a good man.'

'And if we're not?'

'Then I might as well sign the paperwork for an incineration, there isn't a chance in hell I'm paying for his funeral.'

The park of the base was filled with the greenest grass and flowers, trees with real animals in them while the birds flew overhead under the great giant glass ceiling above, so the sun could shine through to brighten the park.

The fountain was the prized wonder of it all, tall statue of a mermaid holding a jar where the water burst from it, pouring out into the basin below, Commander Jim sat on its edge eating his sandwich, having his usual lunch break and enjoying the calm peaceful environment. His lunch today was a tuna sandwich, handmade by his wonderful wife with extra love, yes literally in the way that his wife had the talent for love.

His guest was sitting away, kneeling on the ground and holding a pigeon perched on his arm with every other bird flying or landing around him, looking like he is the one with nature itself. Jim had him cleaned up, bandaged and given new clothes; he rejected the clothes so he gave him an exact spare of the prison clothes he came in with, clean and dry from all the blood which he honestly did not know the store sold those exact ones from the prison he came out of.

Bob stood still as a statue, getting glances from a passer-by who pointed and gasped at his clothing, fearing that a criminal was walking among them, so Jim stood and tipped his fingers off to them to assure their safety from the ex-con. Then, he walked to Bob. 'Impressive, two hours without handcuffs and you haven't tried to escape,' he said.

'Where will I go anyway?' replied Bob in that tone of his, 'The minute I get up you are going to shoot me with your gun,' he added looking at the colt python buckled at his waist.

Jim chuckled, finishing off his sandwich. 'Ah, you have noticed,' he pulled out his gun, showing off its every angle so he could see it, 'This bad boy can blow a chunk out of anyone, especially someone with a talent.'

'You can make the bullets fire faster and stronger,' Bob said.

'How did you know?'

'Lucky guess.'

Jim chuckled. 'Well, my lunch break is over,' he said, Bob stood up as well, turning to see the gun pointed right at his face, Jim held the trigger and pulled back the thumb to aim directly at his nose. Bob tensed and glared at him from the barrel, 'You are right, my talent can increase the durability and speed of the weapon, mostly a gun's range and power by ten times its normal rate, you can run as fast as you can but you will never escape my range.'

Bob stood still, not moving or attempting to flee. 'So what is this, giving me a head start while you shoot me for sport? I don't think doing it in front of all these witnesses is a good idea,' he said.

Jim nodded, 'The people here are either workers or families of the taskmasters, besides you are wearing a prison uniform so while they wouldn't blink an eye anyway, it's perfectly normal for a cop to shoot an escape con.'

Bob stood firm, his eyes on the wavering gun held in his face, Jim waved the barrel side to side, 'There's a gun in your face, yet you are giving me the rudest glare ever,' he pulled the thumb down deeper, ready to pull the trigger under his finger, 'I am going to shoot you at least do something instead of standing there.'

'I'm not worried,' he just said raising a finger to the gun, Jim raised his eyebrow in confusion, 'You got no bullets in that thing.'

Jim smirked, 'You can see the barrel?'

'They're empty.'

Jim chuckled, letting go of the thumb and put the gun away, 'Very well, you have passed the test, hurray for you,' he cheered silently doing a little clap.

Bob just glared at him, slightly taken aback by this sudden result, 'Just like that you're not going to shoot me?'

'Of course, I was going to shoot you, if you had fought back or attempted to flee, then you would be dead on that nice flower bed and I would get someone to incinerate your corpse, no way I'm paying for your funeral.'

Bob lowered his glare, 'What was the point of this stunt then?'

'It would show me the kind of man you are, I plan different scenarios of how this would've turned out, if you hit the gun out of my hands I would use my knife to stab you,' he pulled out the knife behind his back to show him that he is serious, 'Then I would pick up my gun and shoot you anyway, but nonetheless you stood your ground and showed no sign of fear or desperation which to be honest is lacking these days with people,' he held out his hand, Bob grabbed it and held tight, 'You have honour Mr Stewart, and a man with crazy balls as yours to go after the guardians, well, that's all right in my book,' he told him shaking his hand.

'Thank you,' said Bob shaking it back, 'So does that mean you're not going to kill me?'

'Nonsense, not unless you give me a reason to,' he said coldly, then chuckled and let go, 'Let me buy you a drink mate, it's the least I can do,' he slapped his shoulder and led him away from the park. The two men walked to the nearest pub down the road at the Drunken Wagon, a local pub for soldiers to enjoy a nice cold one with their mates.

They entered, seeing soldiers, workers and even lawyers having a chat and drinking, playing pool or throwing darts, this is where all the people who work here come to have a drink. Jim and Bob walked to the bar and sat on the soft stools, 'Carla! Two beers for me and my mate here,' he called out to the waitress slamming his hand on the bench.

The woman sighed and took out a pencil out of her short black hair. 'Two beers for the A-holes, gotcha,' she said jotting it down and proceeded to get them from the tap, pouring them in while Jim chatted with Bob.

'So tell me, how someone like you ended up in prison?' he asked, the beers being placed in front of them.

Bob took his beer and sipped it. 'Doesn't matter,' he muttered, 'What's done is done, even though it was unfair on me.'

Jim rubbed his five o'clock shadow, 'Well, I heard that you were framed for a murder of a young woman, sweet sixteen and had her whole life ahead of her, what was her name?' he took a gulp from his beer.

'Emma Hawkins,' Bob said blankly.

Jim edged him on. 'What I heard is that you killed her, but meeting you right now tells me that you could be an innocent man who got the short end of the stick,' he said looking at him, 'What really happened that night Bob?' he asked again, like a man worried for his mate.

Bob leaned forward; silence filled the room. The chatter around slowly died out as people noticed the prisoner sitting among them, hoping he'll tell his tale like it's a tradition for a soldier to tell his story of why he's here. Carla cleaned a glass as she too listened to the story he's about to tell. The soldiers sat at their table, the lawyers by the wall listening in, even the workers stood around as they all wanted to hear the tale of the fighting prisoner that sat among them.

Bob began his tale, remembering the day it all went to hell, he could see the scene played out in front of him, his friend, hell the girl he fell in love with. Her blonde hair hangs around her shoulders, her old KISS t shirt worn with her blue jeans, turning around and giving him a smile.

'What's with that look, Bob?'

Bob was sixteen back then with his brown hair long and shaggy, like he just woke up, he had no beard but he wore his long-sleeved shirt along with jeans. 'Just not in the mood,' he said in that tone of his.

On that day they were at Bob's house hanging out in his living room, Bob was told they were going to play video games all day but instead Emma wanted to go to the city, claiming that she found a way for them to have magic.

Emma giggled, flicking his head. 'It's just a few miles in the city,' she said, 'Come on this could be our chance to use magic, wouldn't you want that?'

'Yeah, magic doesn't exist you do know that, right?' he argued, Emma always believed in the supernatural, even go far as to claim that she had seen it in real life. But, of course, Bob was always the sceptic but Emma wouldn't give up; she will prove it to him even if they find themselves at the end of the world.

Emma gave him that adorable smile of hers, the one that even Bob couldn't resist, 'Come on, I promise this will change our lives,' she said giving him the puppy eyes.

Bob groaned, hanging his head back and forth until finally he caved. 'OK fine,' he said getting up from the couch. Emma squealed and gave him a massive hug.

'Thank you, I promise you'll look back on this day and you'll kick yourself for almost missing out Bob,' she said with confidence, turning around and heading towards the door.

Bob could not help but smile a bit, 'Oh and stop calling me Bob,' he said, 'You know I hate that name.'

Emma giggled, 'Why? Bob suits you way better than Robert does.'

They began their journey to Sydney, taking the train since it's the fastest route and neither of them had a license, or a car. You see Emma had trouble growing up. Being the rich girl, her father watched her very closely, she longed for a better life than being the snotty girl with a pedicure.

So, she looked for something better, a new reality with magic and adventures like the ones in her books. She believed that magic existed in this world and she could be one of the most powerful sorcerers alive, and she wanted Bob to join her for he was the only guy who saw her as just a normal girl, no one special.

Bob met her back in high school when they were starting year seven both hitting it off quickly for, they both liked adventure books. Of course Emma told him about the magic world but he would always tell her that it is all make believe but she never believed him.

OK, so, he wasn't the friendliest guy.

Ever since then she went bending over backwards, literally at one point, to prove that she's telling the truth and Bob just went along with it. Of course, he did not hang out with her so she could prove something that he did not believe in, he did it so he could hang out with her.

'Ah, you got yourself a crush there, mate.'

'Oh and how many crushes have you had?'

'They all crush on me, I was a respectable gentleman, aren't I Carla?'

'Sure, and I am the Lindbergh baby.'

'You two wanna hear the story or not?'

'Fine, fine. Continue, lover boy.'

They arrived at Central, Emma was so excited she basically bounced off the train. 'Come on, Bob, we're almost there,' she beamed grabbing his hand and dragging him with her.

'Dammit Emma just be patient, I'm sure whatever it is it isn't going anywhere,' he said following her.

Emma shook her finger. 'Oh, will ye have a little faith,' she said once they left the station, Bob getting his hands back and putting them in his pockets, following Emma down the street. They walked a few miles getting leg cramps along the way.

'How far is this place?' said Bob getting tired.

Emma turned her head to him. 'Just a little longer,' she said turning into an alleyway. Bob followed her in and stood in a big empty space with bins, cats and even a bear, the bear held a boar in its mouth and stared at them while slowly backing away into the shadows hoping they don't notice him.

Bob folded his arms, 'OK, Emma, I'll bite, why are we standing in an alley? This is how people get mugged.'

Emma stood in front of him. 'Well, Bob, you know I've been practising some magic of my own,' she said.

'You mean party tricks, but go on.'

'And I come up with a spell to locate magic users, and I found a really powerful one. If I'm right he or she should appear here in this alley, we can ask him to teach us everything he knows,' she told him in such brightness in her voice.

'Is he gonna appear in this box,' Bob asked sarcastically pointing to a random box by the bins, 'Did you find your father's drugs and how much did you take?'

'It's not like that, I really did it!' she said standing next to him. 'Watch, he will teach us spells beyond your wildest dreams,' she said looking to the empty spot.

Bob sighed. 'Look Emma,' he began. 'I don't think you should believe this stuff,' he said rubbing the back of his head.

Emma looked at him. 'Look, I know that I haven't found anything yet, but this time I really did find something just stay with me please,' she said grabbing his hand.

Bob's heart skipped a beat, he wanted to stay but he could not keep encouraging her. So with a heavy sigh he let go. 'Sorry but you need to face reality, I'm leaving,' he said walking away with his back turned. Emma called out for him to come back with hurt in her voice but Bob hung his head low and kept walking to the end of the alley.

But then a loud boom blew his eardrums. Turning sharply to see Emma standing in front of a fire tornado, 'EMMA!' he called out and ran towards her.

Emma turned her head to him. 'See, I told you this is real,' she said turning back to a figure appearing in the flames. 'This is the guy I told you about, hey!' she waved. 'I'm Emma, that's my friend Bob, we are both eager to learn some magic so can you please teach us?' she said to him. Bob stopped just a few steps from her, unable to believe his own eyes. The figure stepped forward, it was a man with a long black beard and covered head to toe in medieval golden armour, the shoulder plates and chest and the iron boots gleamed in the sunlight. He held a sword in his hand, long and pulsing with golden energy. Bob knew the second he saw him he wasn't good, he called out to Emma to run but she did not hear him. 'Hey, did you hear me?' she just yelled to him.

'No mortal can ever be what I am.'

His sword pierced through her, sending a bit of blood on Bob's face, watching Emma get sliced apart.

Chapter 9

'Carla, another beer,' said Jim.

Carla smiled. 'Sure, would you like me to throw it in your face or spill it in your pants?' she said pouring him a glass.

'I'd rather take the glass, thank you.'

Carla placed it in front of him, giving him the finger while she walked to the other customer. 'Popular guy, ain't ya?' Bob chuckled taking another sip of his third glass.

'Oh that's just Carla, still pissed that I slept with her sister,' said Jim.

'Damn, seriously?'

'Oh yeah, but I think the people hear what they wanna hear, more of your story than mine anyways,' he said looking around the room.

Bob turned to see all eyes were on him, the music not playing anymore and people putting their cards away wanting to know what happened next. Bob chuckled to himself, 'Feels like I'm in a western movie,' he took one big sip then he continued, 'Well, you could say the crap hit the fan from there.' Emma split apart on the ground, the light faded from her eyes quickly once she hit the ground in her own pool of blood. Bob fell to his knees, too weak to stand and shaking like the cold just washed over him. 'Emma…' he said softly, he could have stayed maybe he could have saved her but he did not, he banged his fists on the ground cursing and blaming himself for what happened.

The Sorcerer walked towards him with his armour bulky and clanked with each step. Bob looked up at him, tears falling down his cheeks but had rage in his eyes and growled at him. The sorcerer looked down, not saying a word he pulled out the sword and held it high over his head.

'Heh, come on, give me a look of fear,' he said coldly, 'I love it when you humans do that, the realisation of your death is fun to watch,' Bob just glared up at him. 'Aw, that isn't the look I want,' he chuckled pulling his sword down, 'You humans want power for nothing, going to the point where you walked willingly into a trap, see I knew I was being tracked so I made sure that the first mortal to die will be someone who thinks they can have what us gods have.'

'Why?' was all Bob could say.

The sorcerer looked down at him, 'For fun, I love nothing more than to take away the hope from a desperate human,' he raised his sword high, 'I came here to kill, to make this city my kingdom, seeing torment will be the foundation of our new world along with your skull,' he held it back up and thrusted it down towards his head.

Bob kneeled there feeling time slowed down, the girl he had a crush on cut in half and dead because he did not stay, he hung his head ready to die right there in that alleyway.

'BOB!'

Her voice boomed in his head making him jump out of the way of the sword blurring past him, missing him by a hair. Bob got to his feet and got himself ready to fight.

The sorcerer laughed, holding his sword on his shoulder. 'What is this? You are actually going to fight me?' he said, 'Never have I seen such pathetic display of desperation, you actually believe you will live after this.'

'I don't believe. I know,' grunted Bob.

He smiled, 'Allow me to introduce myself, seeing as you won't live long enough to memorise it, I am Kald, one of the guardians', who watch over the mortals.'

'I don't care.'

Kald grinned, holding his sword with both hands he charged at him, faster than Bob had ever seen but he bent backwards like dodging a ball speeding at him, except it was the tip of the sword slicing the air over him. He barrel rolled to the left but the sword swung again at such speed to the ground, slicing his arm in the process. Bob held his arm and fled to the far side of the open space feeling the blood dripping down his arm.

'First blood goes to me,' Kald mocked, licking the blood off his sword and licking it over his blood-stained teeth, 'Mmmm, tasty.'

Bob ripped a strand of his shirt and used it as a bandage for his wound. Then he stood up in a battle stance wishing he had a weapon of some kind, but all he could do was go through his pockets for some keys to use for his knuckles. He rummaged around his phone and wallet, god how he could use a baseball bat right about now.

His fingers wrapped around something, something long and wooden. Feeling a strength of hope he pulled, eyes widen with shock at the baseball bat was pulled out of his pocket. 'Whoa, what the?' he said unable to believe it, did he lose that much blood already? The baseball bat was steel, just as he imagined it but it is here in his hands real and ready to bash someone's head in.

He took a stance, Kald mocking him, 'A bat? You are going to die so wouldn't you want something a bit better?' he took his stance, 'I'm gonna cut you in two just like that dumb girl.'

Bob yelled and charged holding the bat up and swung it down onto his helmet, he did not block or anything the bat just smashed into splinters upon impact. Yes, it was metal so you can understand the shock he had on his face.

Kald swung his sword again but Bob jumped back, the blade slicing across his chest and opened a deep wound, he pressed his palms on it so he wouldn't bleed out. If he falls, he will be killed on the spot, that guy was not messing around. The sword came again but he jumped again to miss it. 'Come on, mortal!' yelled Kald, 'Just accept that you are no match for me.'

Bob huffed, he needed something to break that damned armour of his.

'You cannot surpass my armour,' Kald said like he was reading his mind, 'This armour is forged by the fires of dragons, made with steel of the strongest 'vibranium' titanium and held in the armoury of the guardians for generations, nothing can break me,' he raised his sword back in his stance, 'So come at me, as you mortals say.'

Bob glared, he was really fighting a sorcerer, Emma was right and he did not believe her, and now she's dead. Reaching into his pocket, he prayed for her forgiveness, imagining the armoury he said with the weapons to help him break that armour and kick his ass. He felt her hand holding his and pulled.

Now it was Kald's turn to look shocked, Bob had pulled out a golden giant Hammer made with the same material that made his armour. Kald only saw this back at the Mountain so how did this mortal get it, let alone have it inside his pocket since it is as tall as a frickin' mountain!

Bob stomped his foot forward using all his strength to hold the hammer, he only had one shot to make so he better make it count. He held it over his body, hands spread apart to carry the massive weight feeling it about to crush him to dust. Holding it tight, he screamed and threw it down, the huge metal sped towards Kald who yelled trying to run but the tip of the hammer just smashed right into his head, crushing the helmet in the process he went down fast and got crushed by the massive steel slamming on top of him like a hammer to a roach.

Both the armour and hammer burst into shards of metal that flew everywhere. The walls and the ground and one impaled Bob in the shoulder. He walked to Kald grunting and pulling it out, blood dripping out of the wound.

Kald gagged and coughed out blood, his armour is in pieces exposing his body to the air leaving him vulnerable. He looked up at the victor. 'Do it,' he whispered, 'End me like I ended your girl.'

Rage surged in Bob, his hands clenched together that drew blood, all he wanted was to end his life like he ended hers, he was going to use whatever left of his sword to cut him in half. He held his breath, picking up the sword he held it high, in a stabbing motion he brought it down…

And stabbed the ground next to his head. Kald looked up at him, 'No,' was all Bob could say, if he killed him then how is he better, 'I am not like you,' he stood; leaving the sword standing there and walked away, pulling his phone out to call the police.

He was about to dial when he heard sirens out on the street, looking up to see two cops running in, brandishing guns out right at Bob. 'Hands behind your head!' they called out.

'Thank god you're here, that guy killed…' He turned to show them the body but he was nowhere to be found, where the hell did he go?

'I said put your hands behind your head!'

Bob turned back, the situation slapping him in the face, a girl chopped in half, the sword buried ahead with his fingerprints, hell he had her blood on him of course they're going to assume he did it. 'I did not kill her,' he said shaking. The cops moved closer preparing to shoot him so to avoid that outcome he got on his knees, dropping his phone and putting his hands behind his head. Everything went silent while the cop put his hands in handcuffs, his buddy calling in the crime scene; then he was escorted to the squad car.

The day's events heavy on his mind, breaking down in tears he hit his head on the back of the driver's seat.

The story hung in the air while Bob drained the rest of his beer, while Jim was on his third. 'Mate that's a load of bullshit, did they not investigate? Find the guardian at least?' he said clearly drunk at that point.

'Yeah, I was hoping you could fill that part in, since Wolfe said he was with a group that arrested him, so I'm assuming you were involved as well,' Bob told him.

'Oh right,' he cleared his throat, 'Well, from what we gather at that point Kald managed to drag his body quickly away before the cops came, it was then we found him,' he explained turning to him, 'Taking advantage of his defeat, we isolated him and locked him up, he now resided in a maximum prison in Antarctica.'

'And about this first guardian, where is he locked up? I was told it is somewhere no one could enter without a sort of key.'

'Ah, he is a different matter,' Jim said, putting his glass down, 'He isn't the first guardian, but THE guardian, he's the master of all magic,' he then began telling him the story, 'The taskmasters all stood up and locked him away for all eternity, so he will never use his powers for evil.'

'Just like that?'

'Yep, did not put up a fight, it was quite funny.'

'What did he do?'

'Excuse me?' asked Jim.

'What did he do that made you lock him up?' said Bob.

'Well, so he doesn't use his great ancient magic to kill the world,' Jim told him.

'But did he do anything that proves that?' Bob said back, 'Did he destroy a city?'

'Well, no.'

''Cause Genocide?'

'He did not.'

'Kick a puppy?'

'I don't think so.'

'Did he so much as make a rude comment on YouTube,' he grunted getting annoyed now, rubbing his eyes in frustration.

'OK, so we may have overreacted a tad bit...' Jim said feeling kinda stupid right now.

'You do realise that his brothers are going to release him to kill the world now, right?' Bob told him.

'It was a good idea at the time.'

'So I ask yet again, what the actual hell?! Who's the frickin' moron who decided to lock him up for something he would or wouldn't do without a proper trial!?' He raised his voice, getting really mad that all this started because they were afraid of a Sorcerer's power.

Jim hesitated, he should not say but the guardian had killed his friend in an attempt to destroy the people who locked up his brother, and now his brothers had decided to follow his lead all because of what they did that long ago that now he started to think was a dumb move, and Bob was the one who suffered for it. Hanging his head low he slowly whispered, 'It was Wolfe.'

Bob stood up, throwing his glass to the wall that barely missed Carla and walked to the door, not saying a word to anyone he stormed out, his anger filling the quiet air around the bar. He walked towards the main hub of the base looking to have a few painful words with Wolfe.

Chapter 10

'Sir you really should stay in bed,' said the nurse.

Wolfe ignored her and buttoned up his shirt, putting on his coat he walked past her, 'I don't need to stay, this matter cannot wait,' he said to her. 'Besides I feel fine,' blood spilled out from a wound in his neck for which he then grabbed a new band aid and covered it up.

The nurse tried to argue but Wolfe walked on ahead, meeting Carly by the entrance of the medical centre wearing a black jacket and blue jeans and wore her ACDC shirt to cover her bandages. 'I really think you should stay in bed, you're really injured,' she said worried about his health. But she knew her mentor can be more stubborn than he wanted.

'Ha! that's what they want me to do, then they charge me extra for the month!' he said adjusting the rims of his coat.

'But doesn't your insurance pay for it…'

'Now we have to see the Boss,' he cut in, waving for a cart to stop in front of them, they sat in the back and began to move, Wolfe leaned back while Carly looked at the buildings, her mind heavy with thoughts. 'Worried about Bob?' asked Wolfe.

Carly quickly shook her head, but the look on his face made her cave. 'Yeah, he doesn't know his way around here and I'm sorta worried that he'll get arrested,' she admitted, 'Or killed.'

Wolfe chuckled. 'Don't worry, I'm sure he's enjoying his stay here,' he told her, 'I'll have someone let him know where we'll be,' the cart stopped, a new passenger stepped in and sat next to them, a tall built gentleman looking at them very closely. Carly could see the veins on his exposed skin under that soldier uniform, while the hat held back the long brownish hair that hung behind his head.

The soldier saluted them. 'Greetings, I am Elkcim, I have been assigned to escort you by my commander,' he told them.

'Jim must think we let a criminal in to kill him,' mumbled Carly to Wolfe.

'Well, I see,' said Wolfe nodding. 'Very well if having you proves we are not up to anything, then go right ahead but pretend you are not here,' he told the soldier as the cart moved again, 'Just fade in the background like you're a background character on TV.'

Elkcim nodded, sitting straight with his palms on his tone knees. This guy was twice Wolfe's size, Carly could not believe her eyes, but hey it's a crazy world. They moved through the street until they came to the big dome like building in the centre of it all, the hub.

Wolfe, Carly and their new guest stepped out. 'You know since you invited yourself with us, you should pay,' said Wolfe walking off quickly before he gets a say.

Elkcim mumbled taking his wallet out and paid the driver, then he caught up with Wolfe and Carly. They entered the huge double sliding doors that opened the cool air conditioner hitting their faces. The hub was busy as always with the taskmasters and apprentices taking jobs off the main job board in the centre, where the information desk was also located. The big open area is surrounded by hallways and pathways, elevators and vehicles for easy access. Carly remembered the countless times she and Wolfe came to the hub back in London, it was a lot like this except there were more police telephone boxes.

They walked to the reception desk, Wolfe telling the girl they were here to see the Boss. She nodded and made a few calls letting the boss know that the guests were coming. At that point, Wolfe and Carly headed to the elevator with their soldier buddy following behind. They took the elevator up to the final floor, the main office and penthouse of the boss of the Australian Hub. Each hub had a boss that watched over it, and Guests from other hubs such as Wolfe and Carly from the London Hub, had to let the Boss know of their business in their territory.

Carly shifted her feet, she only knew one boss and one boss only, King Louise, and yes he did call himself that; a strict bloke and the best of the taskmasters. She got scared that he'll throw her out the window one of these days just because he would feel like it, so of course she hoped that this boss wasn't like theirs.

The elevator door opened to the brightly lit furnished room. The office had a desk as huge as the round table itself in the middle of the room surrounded by potted plants of different types and species. A woman was watering them by the corner, wearing an apron and long sunflower hat over her suit pants and shirt. She turned her long red hair towards her guests. 'Oh hello,' she said smiling.

Wolfe stepped forward, 'Excuse me ma'am, we are here to see the boss of the Australian Hub,' he told her.

The woman nodded. 'Ah yes, Dingo, right?' she said putting her water can down. 'I'm not sure if you heard but he sadly passed away,' she told them.

'Seriously, when did he die?' said Wolfe.

'Last year, he sadly got drunk and went speed racing through Dublin.'

'Damn, did he crash?'

'Oh, no he was fine, in fact he won,' she pointed at the trophy case showcasing a gleaming gold race car trophy, 'Once he came back he was attacked by a rabid bear that jumped out of nowhere,' she then pointed at the picture atop the trophy case, showing Dingo getting mauled by a bear in his bathroom. Carly had so many questions at that point.

'Well, that explains why he never came to poker night,' mumbled Wolfe walking around the office. 'So, who's in charge now?' he asked looking at the fly eater plant which just gave him a wink.

'That would be me,' the woman told them, going to the desk while taking off the hat and apron, 'Ivy Violet, the boss of the Australian Hub,' she introduced herself.

Carly giggled to herself, Wolfe cursing under his breath. 'Well, my apologies, if I had known you were the Boss...' he started.

'Don't worry Taskmaster, I knew that none of the hubs got the memo, or if they did, they wouldn't tell their Taskmasters anyway,' she said sitting down, giving them a proper meeting she gestured them to take a seat. Wolfe and Carly took the seats in front of the desk while Elkcim stood by the elevator leaning back his arms folded, 'Now that we got that out of the way, May I ask why I have London's finest walking my countryside?' she asked getting down to business.

Wolfe cleared his throat, 'Well, we are on a mission, you no doubt heard about the guardians planning to eliminate the mortals,' she nodded, 'We believe they are trying to free their brother so they can use his magic to achieve their goal.'

Violet nodded, 'Yes, I have been keeping track of your battles, more notably the battle at the café, how did you manage to defeat and kill that guardian?'

'Well, that wasn't us,' Wolfe told her.

'Yes, I know, I'm talking about your companion the prisoner that you bailed out,' she pulled out a file and read it out loud, 'Robert "Bob" Stewart, age nineteen and imprisoned for the brutal murder of Emma Hawkins, age sixteen at the time,' she turned to them with a certain glee in her voice, 'I did not know you work with serial killers, nowadays.'

'Oh, that's the thing, he's innocent it was a big misunderstanding,' he said.

'I don't care, they say prison changes a man so how would you know he won't kill you and your partner.'

'He saved our lives!' said Carly.

Violet turned to her. 'Stay out of this kid, the grownups are talking,' she told her.

'Oh, you stuck up…'

'Bob has proven himself time and time again that he is not what he appears to be,' Wolfe cut in, 'He was the one who has defeated all three guardians up to now.'

Elkcim tensed his knuckles and growled, Carly could hear a breath of rage coming from him but she's too mad at this old hag to care.

Violet folded her arms, 'Maybe, but have you considered that he wanted you to trust him? Killers like him are insane and brilliant.'

'He's not a killer,' mumbled Carly rubbing her sore belly.

Wolfe slammed his fist on the table. 'Whether we can trust him or not is our business, right now we need to know where the key is,' he said.

Violet looked at him with a glare in her eyes. 'The key is safe, why does it matter?' she said sternly.

'The guardians are coming after it we can help you protect it, I'll make some calls to have it delivered to somewhere secure.'

'The key is secured,' Violet told him, she reaches into her blouse and deep in her chest, pulling out a chain necklace, tied at the end is a solid gold key.

'Is that the key to the first guardian?' Carly asked looking at it with wide eyes.

'No this is the key to my make-up kit,' she said using it to open a drawer in her desk, taking out a lipstick and then she reached into a potted plant and took out a rock. 'This is the real key,' she said putting it on the table.

'A rock,' said Carly thinking she must be smoking something.

'The guardian was locked in a limited space between worlds, a gap or a box for your poor mind to rationalise, the taskmasters had made the key into a form of a small rock, ''Cause who will ever think of something so stupid,' she explained applying lipstick to her lips.

'So you think you can protect it from a guardian?' Wolfe asked

'Mr Wolfe, no sorcerer or guardian has ever crossed these halls, trust me when I say that the key is safe,' she told him, 'Now, you two can go back to London and leave us Aussies to our problems, alright?'

Wolfe opened his mouth to argue, getting up from his seat to convince her to let them help so the first guardian could never come back, but of course he never did for Elkcim charged through and grabbed his neck and flung him back, he burst through the wall into the open air, Carly stood up from her chair and called out his name while Violet was grabbed by the soldier. Carly turned to see him holding the rock in his other palm.

'Thank you for the location,' he said coldly holding his fingers tight around her throat, Violet gasped and kicked trying to get free. Carly may have hated the girl but she could not let her die, so she hopped on the table and kicked him in the sides, but he did not feel it practically ignored her while he squeezed tighter, Carly began punching him trying to get his attention.

Violet rolled her eyes. 'Guess I have to save myself,' she said hoarsely grabbing the soldier's head. Carly saw tiny bugs crawling out of her eyes and her mouth in huge swarms! They swarmed into the soldier's mouth making him let go so he could focus on shaking off the bugs and crush some in his mouth. His hat flew off exposing his long hair.

'Mickle,' gasped Violet trying to catch her breath.

Mickle smiled, standing up on the desk with Violet on the ground, Wolfe knocked out outside the office and Carly standing before him, trying to come up with a strategy to defeat him. Wolfe said in order to defeat a guardian you needed to find his weakness but so far nothing had harmed him, did he even have a weakness?

Mickle held the key in his fingers, the rock clenched between the thumb and fore finger, 'To think you mortals have made a key so idiotic that magic users would never come up with,' he chuckled. 'No matter, now that I have the key, I can kill everyone here starting with you,' he pointed to Carly, 'You,' he pointed to Violet, 'And the taskmaster,' he pointed behind to Wolfe.

Carly's body began to shake she had no chance against him; Mickle was the third strongest out of the guardians right under Mr Red. Plus, she could not beat the other two guardians that came after her before, what chance did she have now?

Her thinking time was over for Mickle as he leapt forward, Carly screamed and threw herself off the table, his finger missing her and struck the table smashing it with only a fingertip! *Crap, that would've been my head,* Carly said to herself continuing to dodge each jab of his finger. Mickle laughed to himself, using his other index finger now. Carly moved twice as fast with both hands jabbing at her head, lucky she manage to miss but how long can she keep this up?

An idea popped into her head, using her talent, she controlled the bugs that remained on the ground and used them to fly around Mickle. 'The bugs, please,' he said, 'Your boss could not stop me with them.'

'Not trying to stop you,' Carly told him, reaching up to grab the rock from his pinky and ring finger, 'Trying to distract you mate,' she yanked it off and began running, heading for the emergency stairs she bolted through and ran down the flights with the roar of the guardian ringing through her ears, but she did not dare look back.

She reached the lobby, people turning to see the girl running through holding a rock for dear life until she bumped and crashed into a person.

'Damn it, Carly!'

Carly got up, looking to see Bob getting to his feet, 'Bob! Oh, thank god!' she said actually glad to see him which was a first.

Bob held up his hand. 'You do not talk; did you know Wolfe was in charge of falsely locking up the first guardian?' he asked sounding really pissed.

Carly was taken aback, 'Falsely? Bob the guardian was going to destroy everything.'

'Was he?!' he yelled.

Carly had no words, the fear and panic from the guardian attack was messing with her head, oh that's right, 'Bob can we talk about this later?' she pleaded.

'No! I wanna talk about this now!' he yelled actually making her terrified, 'My friend is dead because of what your mentor did!'

At that moment the ceiling burst open, Mickle jumping from above and landed in the centre, smashing the board under his feet. He stood up and spotted Carly by the end, looking at her with his own rage-filled eyes.

Bob looked at him and back to her. 'Oh hell,' he sighed grabbing her arm and bolting himself with Carly dragging behind, 'OK fine, we'll talk later about this later!' he called back to her.

Carly smiled, following his lead just as Mickle began his chase.

Chapter 11

Bob and Carly ran through the street the rock clutched in her hands while the guardian chased them with blood in his eyes. All the taskmasters back at the hub tried to subdue him but he proved too strong and flung them all without a second thought to get to his targets.

Bob turned his head to see him pouncing from toe to toe catching up to them fast. So, he bent down to grab Carly's legs, 'Hey, what are you doing?' she began blushing being bridal carried by him, now running faster with her in his arms. She held on to his shoulder her face going red now, she really did not expect this nor did she expect Bob to pull her over his shoulder and hold her by her thigh now so he could reach into his pocket.

'HEY!' yelled Carly now banging his back, looking forward to see Mickle running faster now towards them. 'You better have a good reason for this Bob!' she yelled back to him.

'Shut up and let me think!' he yelled back reaching around in his pocket. Finally, he grabbed something and pulled out a machine gun, long and huge. He stopped and turned shooting an endless barrage of bullets.

Mickle laughed and ran through them, the shells bouncing off his skin like he's superman running in a marathon of flowers. Using one hand he sent a right hook right into Bob's jaw, blood gushing out while he flew back and hit the wall, cracking it and his ribs. Lucky Carly flew off to the side before she was impacted into the wall, 'Stupid mortal, no gun or weapon can harm me.'

Carly got to her feet, the rock still in her hand she turned to see Bob unconscious by the wall, blood dripping down his head. 'Oh, no,' she said softly turning her head to see Mickle charging right at her. She ducked right under him and ran the other way.

The siren blazed through the hub, Violet must have sounded the alarm so civilians could either evacuate or fight back so all she had to do is buy time for more taskmasters to catch up to her, 'cause she was not ready for a fight with a guardian. She ran as much as her legs could carry her but she suddenly felt a sharp pain in her shoulder, staggering she looked and found a piece of metal lodge in her shoulder blade. She looked back to see the guardian jumping high in the air clutching more shards in his hands, 'Give me a break.'

He threw all shards at her with full force. All pointing and speeding like bullets that they would soon be like raining spikes pouring down at her. Carly ran behind a car hearing them hit it until the side is nothing but dents. 'That would've been my head right now,' she said taking out the shard in her shoulder, 'Great add this to my list of injuries,' she threw it with a clank and got to her feet.

Then the car was lifted off the ground, she got a chill and turned to see Mickle holding it up with two fingers. 'Got you,' he said using a thumb to get a grip so he could throw it down. Seeing as she won't make it if she jumps forward, she jumps back instead, hitting his chest but barely missing the car smashing on the ground. Mickle took this chance to grab her hair and hold her up. She kicked and screamed, but not letting go of the rock.

He held her tighter. 'Give me the rock, or do I have to rip your hand off?' he said going for her hand. Carly grunted and activated her talent, calling out to the pigeons nearby at the park. The birds heard her call and all flew in formation, over the gates they flew towards Mickle, who spotted them and tried to hit them away. A distraction enough for one pigeon to grab the shard and put it in Carly's other hand which she then used to cut the hair, the guardian was holding. She landed on her feet and ran past him towards the park. The guardian let out a roar, he swiped the birds out of his path and chased after her.

She ran towards the fountain with a plan to cut through it and lose him in the trees. Well, she made it to the fountain but only because Mickle burst off the ground and aimed a foot into her back. The foot cracked her spine and sent her spiralling into the side of the fountain, right on the concrete that burst water and blood everywhere while she fell face first into the basin. Gasping for air, she got up in the water that was still around her but was also spilling out onto the pavement. Her back was in so much pain, she could not move anymore so she laid herself back on the statue. She groaned with each movement of her shoulder blades but quickly looked at her hand seeing the rock is still there.

Mickle took a mighty laugh, 'You are quite the runner mortal but this game is over,' the water from the fountain was still spilling, running along the ground where she was sent flying. Mickle put one foot just before the puddle, 'I am going to take that Key from your lifeless corpse, then I will kill everyone here,' he proclaimed, the puddle moving onto his foot now.

Suddenly, his foot began to smoke, and then Mickle let out a yelp of pain lifting up his foot which the skin on it was burning like it touched the sun itself. Carly watched him take a step away from the puddle like his life depended on it.

Water.

Carly got onto her feet, 'That's water!' ignoring the pain she bent down and held her hands under the water, throwing them up so the water can splash onto the guardian. Mickle got drenched but burnt by the very drop that fell onto him. Cursing and growling at her now but not worried for one bit for he and Carly knew that if the water in the basin goes empty, it won't take long for him to walk in and snap her neck. He ran now to the rocks by the side of the pathway. Carly watched him closely as he picked up a rock and chucked it. Not at her but at the side of the basin with such force it burst, spilling all the water out of the fountain now.

Carly's heart began to pound looking at the water draining down to her ankles, soon she will be defenceless. She looked around for something to do with the water but she needed at least enough water to burn him to a crisp. The water at the huge hole now leaving the ground bare but luckily she spotted a hose attached to a tap by the tree behind her, the perfect weapon. With no hesitation to the pain in her back she bolted towards the hose but Mickle sped towards her, manoeuvring around so he can stand in her path, 'No more games!' he said with such fury grabbing her head with both hands. Going on instinct she spit in his face burning the tip of his nose. Then in pure desperation she struck out her tongue and blew a raspberry getting spit all over his face before he could crush her skull.

It was enough for him to let go and grab his own face to stop the burning, Carly then half ran/half limped to the hose seeing it

91

as her only chance to get out alive. She heard the guardian's roar behind her making her look back to see him fuming with rage now, looking at her with what's left of his face since his eyeballs were exposed with no eyelids, jaw melted on one side and half his skull exposed by the cheek. Damn, her spit really did that much damage?

Carly took a step back keeping one eye on him and one eye at the hose. She could not open the hose and defend herself at the same time, he'll get her before she turned on the tap. Taking a breath she decided to take the risk. So, she turned and ran reaching the hose with her hand and ducked, landing on the ground expecting a hit from behind. But there never was one.

Mickle was being held back by a rope lassoed around his neck which is being pulled by Bob covered with blood but still standing. Mickle gagged trying to pull the rope off with his hands but Bob held on tight so he would be bent backwards, Carly saw this as a chance to turn on the hose, turning and opening the tap she heard the water run through the hose. Then she stood and aimed it at the guardian.

But no water came out. Carly panicked and began to shake and hit the nozzle, 'It's not working!' she called out to him.

The guardian broke the rope and went for Carly but Bob jumped on his back and got him in a full nelson, 'Turn the nozzle!' he yelled out at her getting Mickle locked in place.

Carly grabbed the edge and turned. A burst of water blasted from the end soaking them both, Mickle screamed under the water burning like he was engulfed in lava. The only thing Bob had to worry about was drowning in the water. The guardian let out an ear-piercing scream while his skin melted, eyes bulging out he slipped out his bony arms out from Bob's arms, leaving a puddle of blood, skin and bones under him and left a red muscled corpse.

She turned off the hose and dropped it at her side. Bob drenched from head to toe in water and blood, and bits of skin at his arms. He kicked the guardian's head then walked to Carly, 'Damn, that was close,' he said to her.

Carly nodded holding up the rock to make sure it is still there, 'I just defeated my first guardian,' she said breaking the tension.

Bob did not look at her, 'So did we almost die for a rock?' he grunted clearly still mad about something, oh yeah, that's right.

'Bob,' she started, 'Whatever Wolfe did he probably did it for a good reason,' she tried to explain, but truth be told she did not believe it herself.

Bob just turned and walked away from her, 'I got nothing to say to you but a lot to say to your mentor,' he said leaving her feeling hurt a bit. But then suddenly a hand grabbed her arm. She yelled out turning her head to see Mickle using the last of his strength to snatch the Rock from her hand. Bob heard her and turned and charged at them but Mickle threw her into him knocking them back onto the ground. He then stood and opened a portal, falling in while it closed behind him leaving Bob and Carly sitting up on the ground. Carly sat up and swore under her breath.

'How could you let him escape with the key?!' yelled Violet swinging her arm in a sling while the workers were fixing the damages to the hub. Bob and Carly stood with her with Carly feeling ashamed while Bob just ignored them, both having his hands in his pockets and standing really cool.

Wolfe walked up to them, 'Leave them Violet, from what I heard they won the battle,' he said making Carly smile a bit at that achievement.

Violet groaned putting a hand to her forehead, 'That key was guarded very well until you three showed up at my doorstep!' she grunted.

Bob glared at Wolfe, 'Guess you should've thought of that before you condemned an innocent man,' he said addressing Wolfe only.

'Hey are you ignoring me!' Violet snapped going up to him, 'Who the hell are you anyway!' she demanded putting a finger to his chest trying to get his attention, 'Hell, I bet you let him get away just to get us back right? Jim told me what happened at the pub,' noticing that Bob wasn't paying attention she slapped him across the face, 'HEY! Look at me when I'm talking you!'

Bob turned sharply at her, 'SHUT UP YOU'RE ANNOYING!' he yelled to her.

'I BEG YOUR PARDON!' she yelled back going to slap him again but getting a feeling from his eyes that if she tried, she wasn't going to get her hand back. So she swallowed her anger and lowered her hand, 'Fine, fine. I guess I'll have to fix this mess then,' she grumbled walking away.

Carly watched her leave feeling uneasy when she turned to see Bob and Wolfe resuming their staring match.

Wolfe sighed, 'So you found out.'

'Yeah, you can really make a man talk when he had a few beers,' Bob said, 'So is this what you taskmasters do? Lock people up because they might use their powers for evil?'

'Bob I think Wolfe had a very good reason…' began Carly trying to calm things down.

'I did not,' Wolfe said, 'I was afraid of his power so I made a team to help me capture and lock him in a place where he won't get out and I would do it again,' he added getting his point across.

Bob tensed his fist, 'So what happens if Carly becomes too powerful? You saw her power and experienced it yourself so are you going to lock her up too?' he asked, 'or what about me? What happens if I get out of your control?'

'I'm right here you know.'

'Carly is still my student so it is my duty to teach her the difference between good and evil, she will be a powerful taskmaster who will protect this world,' Wolfe answered with that cool confidence of his, 'But answer me this Bob, when you found out about what I did, the part I played in your friends death, you were so angry not just at me but all of us yet you rescued my apprentice and fought the guardian, why?' Bob turned away refusing to look him in the eyes, 'I tell you why, 'cause you can't turn a blind eye while someone's life is in danger, if someone is going to die you stepped in no matter your personal feelings at the time so no one can die just like Emma did.'

'How dare you?' he growled.

'I did what I did to protect this world from the dangers lurking in the shadows the same as any taskmaster,' he continued, 'You can sleep soundly at night knowing that we are the ones holding back them back,' he turned his back on him, 'Now, if you're done, we need to stop the guardians from opening the prison, so time is now an issue here, there's a garage at the end where we came in,' he pointed out the door to the entrance of the Base, 'Carly and I will proclaim a vehicle and chase them, lucky, I know where the prison is,' he turned back, 'We'll be leaving in an hour, If you want to do more right by your friend then meet us there, otherwise you have no obligation to us,' he left the hub.

Carly looked at Bob then to Wolfe. Knowing she might regret this she went up to him, 'If I'm going to be honest, I'm thankful you saved me,' she said before going after Wolfe, 'Sorry,' she said finally to Bob before running out and started walking beside her mentor towards the garage. Bob being left alone with his thoughts.

They walked in silence towards the Garage where the vehicles of the hub were parked. The plan is to take one of the cars and chase after the guardians before they released their brother from his prison.

Carly did the math in her head; there were eight guardians all together at the start. The First is imprisoned so it's down to seven. Drybon was defeated and killed at the café so that's six. Mozart was defeated as well and she did not forget the guardian that Bob defeated years ago so that brings it down to four.

Four guardians to fight, sure like that won't be a problem.

'Something on your mind?' asked Wolfe breaking the silence.

Carly shook her head, 'Just counting the enemies we have left to fight,' she told him.

'Don't forget, if they release the First then we have a God to face,' he reminded her.

'Don't remind me,' she moaned, now that would be five. She turned her head a little to look behind her.

Wolfe turned his head to her, 'You still thinking about Bob?' he asked.

Carly sighed and turned back, 'I know he's a prick, but he did save my life without him I would've been dead, hours ago.' she held her bandaged hand. Her back still stinging from the impact, lucky the medics managed to heal her spine before it became permanent otherwise she wouldn't even be able to walk for a few days, 'I admit when I was facing that guardian alone I was afraid,' she admitted, 'But seeing Bob fighting without hesitation kind of inspired me to do the same.'

'Yeah, he does have that effect,' chuckled Wolfe.

She smiled, 'Well, there's no point in thinking we'll see him again, considering he hates your guts now.'

'Hey, he hates you too.'

'Nah, if it was you who were fighting, he would've just left you there.'

Wolfe put a finger to his chin, 'Maybe you have a point there.'

'I think he has a talent,' she said, 'During the fight I saw him pull out a machine gun from his pocket, and I'm talking about a huge machine gun,' she used her hands to show him the size, which was really big by the distance she made, 'Do you think he can become a taskmaster as well?'

'I had a feeling he is one, it would explain all the bizarre items he managed to acquire,' he nodded, 'It should be quite possible, after all he has fought powerful enemies and won each time,' he said.

'And, now, that will never happen thanks to you,' Carly said giving off a cheeky smile.

'Are you saying it's my fault?'

'Kinda.'

They arrived at the garage before Wolfe could argue back. A big building with an open hanger door in the back that lead to the outside lined by rows of cars, trucks and airplanes. They stopped right at the entrance, Wolfe taking a look back and scanning the area behind them. In the distance people were re-entering the headquarters once the alarm sound gave the all clear to enter.

'Looks like he's not coming,' he said.

Carly lowered her head actually feeling a bit disappointed, 'Fine, let's go,' she said turning to walk inside, they didn't need him anyway it's always been her, and Wolfe and they got out of situations like these all the time. Suddenly, she got a chill in her spine; she turned around forming a smile on her face.

Bob walked down the path towards them having his hands in his pockets, his prison jumpsuit washed and the blood wiped off his skin. Wolfe folded his arms chuckling at his sense of time, 'You're late,' he told him once he entered the warehouse.

'Had to clean myself up,' he explained, 'Also the tiny fact of I did not know where this place is.'

'It's a huge garage!'

'Do you know how many huge garages they have in this place?!'

Wolfe just grinned and held out his hand, 'So we're good?' he asked him.

Bob looked at his hand then back to him. Carly beaming like the sun itself expecting Bob to take his hand and shake, signalling their understanding towards each other and going back to being a team. As on cue, Bob took his hand out of his pocket…

And punched Wolfe straight on his nose while wearing an iron glove on his hand.

Wolfe cursed out loud and covered his nose trying to stop the blood flowing out, 'Yeah we're good,' Bob told him taking his glove off and chucking it away, 'So you better have a decent car to drive this time otherwise we are walking,' he continued.

And once again Carly hates his guts, 'You Jerk! He was trying to be nice!' she yelled at him.

Wolfe stood up now holding a handkerchief pressed against his nose, 'Actually, I personally had my car transferred here just in case, it's just over there,' he pointed out leading the way with Bob following him leaving Carly to stand there dumb founded.

'Urgh! Men!' she groaned to herself following behind.

They walked up to the car by the end, a shiny black land rover, leather seats and strong wheels for sand travels and a reinforced steel coat guaranteed to protect from missiles at least that's what Wolfe was told when he bought it. Carly and Bob stood awkwardly watching Wolfe rubbing the steel hood.

'Ah, it's good to see you sexy,' he said to the car.

Bob turned his head away while Carly covered her face with her hands, god he can be so embarrassing, 'We got company,' Bob said next to her making her head look up and turn to where he's facing.

Violet came waltzing in with a whole army of taskmasters behind her all marching and forming a circle around the three. Carly stood ready for a fight while Wolfe stopped, "admiring the car", and came up to Violet, 'A going away party for us three, you really shouldn't have,' he said.

'Taskmaster Wolfe you are here by ordered to stand down and come with us, you your apprentice and your companion,' Violet said clearly not sounding like it's a request but a threat.

Wolfe stood calmly, 'We are leaving, if you wanna stop us then by all means be my guest,' he told them, 'Remember that it will be your choice to prevent us from saving the world.'

Violet crossed her arms, 'What are you planning, you three vs the rest of the guardians? Or how about their big brother you gonna beat him as well? Get your head out of the clouds Wolfe,' she said through gritted teeth, 'I am sending my best taskmasters to clean up your mess.'

'They will all die, we have a better chance of winning,' Wolfe said.

'Stand aside, Taskmaster,' Violet said one last time.

Wolfe looked from her to the taskmasters standing behind ready to take them on. He then had begun to figure out a strategy for them all to escape. Option one was he and Bob could take down some of them and Carly could summon birds to attack as well but they would still be outnumbered. Option two was that they get in the car and drive through them but that wouldn't work for he did not know if some of them could take down a car easily. Option three was cry like a little girl and hope they feel awkward enough to let them go.

Option three sounds like a good plan but then a voice boomed out through the garage, 'Hold it right there!'

All eyes turned to the entrance to see Commander Jim walking towards them soon walking past each taskmaster and made his way to the front. He then saluted both Violet and Wolfe, 'As Commander of the hub, I say we let them go,' he said with such confidence.

'Are you serious?!' Yelled Violet in his ear.

'EEEEOOOWWWWW! Not so loud I still have a hangover,' whined Jim putting his finger in his ear, 'Sheesh you have the scream of a banshee from the depths of hell.'

'Explain to me why you are on their side?' said Violet clearly getting on her nerves.

Jim chuckled, ''Cause I honestly think these three have a better chance than we do at this moment,' he told her, 'A guardian has walked in here with no problem and these guys took care of him for us before he did some real damage.'

'Yeah, my spine getting snapped doesn't count as real damage, I guess,' Carly mumbled.

'I think,' he continued ignoring that attitude, 'The least we can do is keep our mouths shut and let them do their job,' he then turned to Bob, 'I had a drink with this man and nothing bonds some mates but cracking a couple of cold ones, so I can tell you that he can beat whatever comes across his path, which is why Bob that once this is over I would like to personally offer you a job here.'

Bob folded his arms, 'Thanks for the offer but I'm gonna pass,' he said.

'I'm not taking no for an answer.'

'OK, get lost you drunk!' he yelled instead.

'Bob, don't insult the man who is helping us,' Wolfe quietly said to him making a motion with his hand.

Jim just laughed, 'Ahahaha! Mate you are something else I tell ya,' he chuckled, 'Alright, get the hell out of here.'

Bob gave a small shrug and got in the back of the rover. Carly stood there more confused than ever but got in the passenger seat, thinking, it's best not to ask. Wolfe looked to the annoyed look on Violets face and smirked getting into the driver's seat.

Jim laughed slapping Violet on her shoulder, 'Don't worry boss, trust me on this one,' he told her then going to the open window just as Wolfe started the car.

'Sure not like you just spent the last hour drinking or anything,' mumbled Violet.

'Listen, I'm going to round up a crew of powerful taskmasters to give you backup, so it might take us time to follow,' he told the trio, 'So if you fail in stopping them at least we got a whole army to deal with the brother.'

Wolfe looked at him, 'Don't worry about it, we can handle them ourselves,' he assured him.

'Oh, I got a feeling but you know my sister hates to not have a backup plan,' he said standing back and giving them all a salute while the garage door opened to the open road outside.

'Good Luck! We are all counting on you!' he yelled.

'Give me a break,' Violet sighed, 'You have got to be the worst brother ever.'

'No way,' whispers Carly under her breath looking at everyone giving them a salute while the car speeds out of the garage.

'Here we go!' yelled Wolfe.

Carly sat back in her seat, Bob in the back folding his arms and closing his eyes for a nap while Wolfe sped along the highway that before they knew it Ayres Rock became a small speck behind them.

Chapter 12

Mr Red sat by the entrance to the tower tapping his foot relentlessly.

The Tower, as the guardians called it since all the good names were taken. Their first choice being Great Rod but that was taken of course. The building was thirty storeys high with a lobby at the bottom and twenty-nine storeys of stairs reaching to the final floor and of course the towers' roof itself. The Tower's design itself is charred black with a long blood red line going around it until the point reached the centre of the top signalling it would be pointing at something in the sky.

Mr Red stood from his seat waiting for his brother to return with the key, for you see he needed it to unlock the prison that had his brother. The eyes under his black sunglasses turned, if you can see it, towards the portal opening up by the door. He walked towards the burning husk of Mickle falling out of the hole. He stood over the gasping burning husk, 'What happened to you?' he asked in that cold voice of his.

Mickle's eyes looked up at him using a mixture of bone and muscle that represented his hand holding up the rock, 'I…got it,' he managed to say, 'The mortals have damaged me but I shall heal soon.'

'So, you have been busted by mortals,' Mr Red just said taking the rock out of his hand.

Mickle coughed up some blood, 'I will not be next time, I shall have that girl's skull in my hands and crush it like a tin can,' he looked up at him, 'I will not let my brothers down.'

'Oh, but you have,' Mr Red said looking down straight at his eyes, taking off his sunglasses, 'What is a guardian that got beaten and killed by mortals?' he told him.

Mickle gasped once he looked into his eyes, his own beginning to glow, 'I can kill them, they just got lucky…,' A sharp pain began growing in his brain rolling down to his heart that it was making him wither in pain. He soon fell onto the ground never taking his eyes off of those damn eyes that were causing the pain. Smoke started to erupt from his ears and eyeballs signalling his brain and heart were melting. Gasping puffs of smoke he had never felt so much of this pain before, especially with the water. His eyes burnt black and then fell into a pile of ashes on the ground that was once his brain and heart, soon Mickle fell into it dead.

Mr Red put his sunglasses back on just when a voice called out, 'BROTHER!'

He turned to see the twins running towards them, the giant muscled one Kane got on his knees, moaning for his fallen brethren behind his long, shaggy red hair that went down around his neck, weeping tears onto his red battle armour.

His twin brother, the heavy built Abel, sighed, his own blue hair tied in a ponytail keeping his eyes cleared as he pulled out a handkerchief to wipe his tears. 'Another fallen brother, oh how the mighty have fallen,' he said in that cool smooth voice of his while his brother had more of a violent growl when he speaks.

'Tell us Brother! Was it the mortals that did this?! That did this to all our brothers?!' Kane yelled out in rage.

Abel turned to Mr Red. 'We found Mozart the same way in a cell,' he told him, 'These mortals are killing us one by one.'

Mr Red nodded, 'Yes, it is a shame but I have news my brothers,' he held up the rock in front of their eyes seeing the look of joy returned in them. 'We finally have the key, I shall prepare the ritual on top of this tower but the mortals are coming,' he warned them, 'You two share only one weakness but it is a weakness they can never exploit therefore giving you an advantage to kill them,' he turned towards the tower door and pushed the great doors open. 'If you can't kill them right away then at least make sure they can never get into this tower,' he said to them before disappearing into the darkness.

'I will rip their hearts out of their skulls!' yelled Kane brandishing his axes out of his back, 'I will use their blood as my own personal river! I will find their loved ones and make them suffer along with them in the depth of hell!'

'Calm down brother!' yelled Abel pulling his sword out. 'We shall defeat them not with anger, but with a calm mind,' he told him.

Kane growled settling down now to calm his mind. Abel talked to him more of what they're going to do while Mr Red walked up the stairs towards the top. He smiled to himself, the mortals had gotten lucky but they had made this tower their domain, therefore, there won't be any weaknesses laying around nor would they be able to defeat them on their home ground. Kane and Abel were the most ruthless guardians out of them, even more so when they lose their temper and when they lose their temper no one will be able to match their combined strength.

He just hoped the tower won't get destroyed at that moment.

The car pulled over to the side of the long bare road. The highway surrounded by nothing but sand and kangaroos hopping about giving off a sense of calm for the trio to take a short breather at the rest stop.

Bob laid on the hood of the car with his hands behind his head. His mind busy by coming up with strategies to beat his upcoming opponents for there were only four left including Mickle who may have healed himself and regained his strength for round two but now that he knew his weakness, he could just grab some bottles of water for the battle.

Carly came out of the toilets, she was not going back there ever again for the spiders seemed to have taken control of the stalls. She walked up to Wolfe looking at the map spread out on the hood next to Bob's legs, 'Here,' he pointed to a spot. 'That is the location of the Tower, where we had the first brother locked up,' he explained to her.

'Could not come up with a better name?' Bob said.

'Well, we wanted to call it the worst name ever known to man, but Woggle tower was taken,' he admitted sarcastically.

'How can you guys be calm about this?' asked Carly actually getting some chills, 'We are going to face four guardians, three we did not meet and a possible fifth god like one and that's if we don't beat them before they release him,' her heart pounded rapidly just by thinking about it.

Wolfe chuckled, 'Do not fret my young apprentice, the higher the enemies to beat, the easier it will be.'

'I don't think, you said that right.'

'Now, over the years the guardians have taken full conquest of the tower so it had now became their turf, So they would expect us to go up the stairs but that would be a horrible idea since they could ambush us in those close quarters, instead of that we are going another way up to the top,' he pulled out a notebook and pen drawing a terrible drawing of a tower then putting a x on the top. 'That is where they will perform the ritual,' he explained, 'Now the ritual they figured it out years ago but never had the key, they tried making one but that did not go so well, now that they have the actual key they can finally unlock the prison, we need to either beat them or get the key before then,' he looked up at them, 'Sounds easy in theory, eh?'

Bob got off the hood putting his hands in his pockets. 'Sure, just add the part where we get ripped or eaten,' he said looking at the horrible drawing, 'So, if we're not going to take the stairs just how else will we get to the top? Did you or the guardians put in an elevator?'

'Bugger off, mate,' Wolfe retorted, 'We are climbing it, of course.'

'Are you serious?' asked Carly starting to think that maybe her mentor is insane, 'How are we going to climb the tower? We don't have any climbing supplies, plus, I am not using my hands I've seen what it does to fingernails.'

'Well, lucky we have our talented guest with us,' Wolfe told her looking at Bob.

Bob raised an eyebrow, 'Me?' he said.

'Yes, your talent, Mr Stewart.'

Bob looked at him with that glare of his, 'So you knew,' he said.

'Well, of course, how else would you get things that are impossible to get.'

'Not Impossible,' Bob said pulling a baseball bat out of his back pocket, 'As long as it exists, I can pull it out, anything that doesn't exist I can't, seeing as I wanted to pull out a time machine many times.'

'Did it work?' asked Carly curious herself.

'I got a photo of a TARDIS, that's close at least,' he chucked it away. 'I did not know anything about this power until you guys told me about it,' he admitted.

'Will you be able to pull out some grappling hooks and climbing gear,' Wolfe asked.

Bob nodded, 'Yeah, I can.'

'Then that is how we will climb the tower, and we'll do it so they won't spot us,' he finished putting his notebook away then rolling up the map. 'Let's hit the road, after I take care of some business,' he said turning to the toilets, Carly wanted to warn him but he already stepped inside the male stalls screaming out, 'OH MY GOD IS THAT A SPIDERS NEST?! WHY DO THEY HAVE WINGS?!'

Bob got back into the car with Carly getting back in the passenger's seat. She turned to him, 'Hey, thank you for saving me back at Ayres Rock,' she said.

Bob just scoffed, 'Don't mention it,' he said, 'That prick would've killed me along with you anyway.'

'You know it wouldn't kill you to at least act like a decent human being,' she told him.

'Maybe, it will.'

Carly groaned turning back, 'You are just so hard to deal with sometimes,' she said quietly.

'Well, after this mess is dealt with, I'm gone.'

Carly's frown got deeper, feeling a bit hurt she exclaimed, 'So, you're not going to stay with us?'

'Why would I want to?' asked Bob looking at her, 'I got some business to take care of.'

'Like what?' Carly asked turning back.

Bob folded his arms, 'My family, I haven't seen them since I was incarcerated,' he hung his head back, 'And I want to apologise to Emma's family, I owed them at least that.'

Carly laid back in her seat. 'I see,' she just said.

Bob looked at her, 'Even if I decide to continue this life what would I do anyway?'

'Well, we could teach you to become a taskmaster like Wolfe,' she explained turning back, 'With your talent you will be a very strong one at that.'

'Not my style.'

Carly groaned, Bob noticed her frustration but there was still something lingering at the back of his mind. Leaning forward he asked quietly, 'What did you mean the guardians killed your family?'

Carly's eyes widened, looking at the expression on his face like he really wanted to know. She looked away and took a deep breath. 'It happened three years ago, back when I was ten years old and started my training under Wolfe,' she started, 'By that year we made so many enemies, stopped so many Sorcerers and Taskmasters alike.'

'They did not know of course, to them Wolfe is my manager in his company and they figured this is a great opportunity for me, it worked and they believed it but one night Wolfe needed me to help track a guardian in the city, so I snuck out, 'cause I did not want them to worry, but when I got back…' She trailed off but Bob could see the painful memory in her eyes, he did not need to know the rest because he could read it on her face. That night was the night the prophecy was foretold among the guardians.

Carly was just a child when she returned to a burning house blazing in the night, finding not her loving parents but a man in golden armour walking out of the flames.

Kald spotted young Carly standing traumatised by the street. 'So there you are, the apprentice of Taskmaster Wolfe,' he said in a dark voice, 'The prophecy said a Taskmaster and his apprentice would defeat the guardians,' he looked down at her seeing the fear on the little's girl face, 'Knowing you and your mentor's reputation, I know that you will stop us, my brothers don't see it now but they will one day.'

He raised a foot and kicked Carly in her face, making her fly back on the ground. The guardian held up his boot over her head. 'I'll kill you and then your mentor, so no one will oppose me,' he chuckled getting ready to throw his foot down until he was knocked back by a chunk of wood powered by electricity. He stood back to see Wolfe standing there clenching his fists that are pulsing with electricity.

'Ah two birds, this will be my night,' he said grabbing out his sword. Wolfe grabbed Carly by her arm and pulled her to her feet. He pushed her behind him to shield her from any attacks Kald might use. But to the golden knight it would be useless but he could sense more mortals coming to the fire, some of them taskmasters.

'Next time, I guess,' he said opening a portal and disappeared into the night.

Wolfe turned towards Carly seeing tears running down her cheeks, not talking or moving a single muscle the poor girl in too much shock to do anything. The only thing a mentor could do is pull her into a hug until the taskmasters arrived at the scene. Carly watched the flames that haunted her to this very day.

The flames still blazed bright in her eyes while she finished the story, 'After that Wolfe tracked him down to Australia to bring justice and to make it up to me, he thinks it was his fault this happened,' she took a breath. 'But when he caught up to him he was beaten and brought close to death,' she finished turning one eye to Bob staring down at the ground, 'After that I was too scared to face anyone stronger than me which is why I wanted to get strong enough to beat the guardians, I planned to kill them all until I met you.'

Bob did not look at her; he did not have to, for he knew how much pain the guardians caused them both.

Wolfe got back into the car with a slam on the door. *Well, it's official, I will never use any toilets in Australia ever again,* he said to himself looking at Carly's sorrowed face and Bob's usual look staring out the window. 'Did I miss something?' he asked them.

'Nothing,' said Carly.

Wolfe shrugged and started the car, driving out of the rest area and down the long empty road once again heading towards the final battle with the guardians. Bob sat in the back now fully understanding his friends' motives for doing this mission. Carly had been haunted by them for three years, losing a part of herself she could never take back and Wolfe wanting to do right by her. All three had their lives changed by the guardians.

Before he never wanted to get involved but now that he realised what this mission meant to them, he made a new goal to free them from their burden.

Chapter 13

The car zoomed across the outback past the hopping kangaroos and running emus. The landscape had gotten dark under the setting sun with the tower rising from the horizon.

It reached as high as the eye could see even from a distance which meant they had a hell of a climb to get through. Wolfe drove them down the small hill crushing the specks of sand under the wheels until finally they arrived at the two big doors where two figures stood by the door waiting for them.

'Well, looks like we're diving straight into this,' said Wolfe.

Bob leaned forward in his seat along with Wolfe and Carly looking out the window. Two knights seemed to be guarding the door, one normal built but still looking very strong with his hair blue and tied into a ponytail with his sword strapped to his back, the other was similar but a little taller with his hair red as blood and falling around his shoulders, he held an axe in his hands ready to chop some heads off.

'These must be guardians,' said Carly.

Wolfe nodded, 'Kane and Abel, the twin brothers of death,' he told them.

'Lovely name,' mumbled Bob.

'So we are going to fight two at the same time,' Carly moaned, it was hard enough fighting one in the first place.

Bob and Wolfe got out of the car first, not wanting to look bad, she got out as well following them towards their opponents. The guardians stood tall watching them walking and stopping just in front of them. 'So you have arrived,' the blue-haired one, Abel said.

'What's our plan now?' Carly whispered to Wolfe.

'Defeat them quick then climb the tower,' he said.

'Easier said than done,' she mumbled.

Bob moved past them. 'Wolfe and I will take care of them, you just have to climb the tower yourself,' he said handing her a grappling gun, 'Once they're distracted, get going.'

'But...' she started but Wolfe already moved past her.

'Do what he says, we'll be right behind you,' he reassured her.

Kane chuckled behind his creepy smile which Abel ignored, watching Bob and Wolfe stand in front of the girl like they were her shields. 'So you two will face us, I must say I thought the killer of our brothers would be more intimidating,' he told them.

'I did not kill anyone,' Bob told them.

'LIAR!' Kane yelled, 'YOU killed Mickle! AS WELL as Mozart and Drybon our BROTHERS!' he spat with rage in his voice.

They're dead? Wolfe said to himself, 'That's impossible we did not kill them or any of your brothers!' he yelled to them.

Kane stomped his foot into the ground sending a mighty quake around them that cracks the hard ground beneath them, 'I will crush you both until your blood fills up the bathtub of my home, AND I shall BATHE IN IT!'

Carly tried not to picture him taking a bath, looking to the guys getting ready to fight she snuck off around them till she's out of sight by the side of the tower, *OK, gotta get to the top, Bob and Wolfe can take care of them,* she said to herself holding the grapple gun upwards she aimed for a ledge or something for the latch to grab on to. But something caught her eye; she looked forward at the wall making a humming noise. *What is that?* she wondered holding a finger to it.

Then got a great electric shock by blue lighting that sent her flying backwards.

She sat up while her hair is a puffy afro being static with leftovers from the shock, *'Urgh,'* her ears were blazing, her head foggy while the world seemed to be moving. She took a minute to rest her head so her vision can return.

Her vision returned just as Bob flew past her and hit the ground far from her with Kane coming down upon him swinging the axe down towards his head. Bob moved quickly out of the way but Kane sent a kick right into his rib, making him cough up blood and received an elbow to the face. Kane got ready to swing again with the intention of not missing his neck.

Carly charged forward and used her shoulder to hit him on the back, it did not hurt him one bit but it was enough to make him lose his aim and miss Bob by an inch. While it did not hurt him, it did hurt Carly's shoulder a lot.

Seeing his chance, Bob grabbed his waist pushed himself off the ground he sent Kane falling on his back and sent punches into his face, but that only made Kane shove the back of his hand into his side, Bob yelled falling off him but getting to his feet just as Carly's eye began to glow.

She called out to any animals in the vicinity, kangaroos heard her call so they bounced and bounced in a stampede together towards their target, the guardian named Kane.

Kane stood with his axe back in his hands raising it up over Bob but was swarmed by angry and hyper kangaroos stomping into him and sending him their own fists. Kane swung at them, chopping some in halves and in a few pieces but the barrage continued.

Bob stood up next to Carly, 'Hey why aren't you climbing?' he asked her.

'The tower shot me back,' she told him.

'Great so they put some spells on it, figures,' he grunted getting into a battle stance. Kane finished off the last of the kangaroos. 'Go see if Wolfe needs a hand, I'll take care of Mr Angry here,' he told her before charging towards him to send a shoulder barge into his belly.

Carly hesitated; looking back she saw Wolfe in his battle with Abel which was not going good as well since Abel was a master swordsman calculating his opponents' next moves and thrusts his sword with such precision. Wolfe used the electricity around his body to move faster than any normal man making him dodge his attacks but barely.

But it didn't look like it's enough, for Abel was getting faster as well, swinging close enough to slice him now, Wolfe had no choice but to jump back and kick off the ground with his talent so he could jump farther. Abel stopped slicing now and held his sword out. 'Give up, Taskmaster, I have killed many like you before, and will continue to do so,' he announced.

Wolfe cracked his neck. 'There is always a first time to everything,' he said doing some calculations of his own but if he just knew his weakness then he could have the upper hand.

Abel's magic is in his sword and speed so powerful magic like that must have a cost but what is it?

The guardian laughed, Wolfe raising his eyebrows at this sudden emotion, 'You are trying to determine my weakness, I shall tell you right now that I have only one,' he told him.

The taskmaster held his guard, 'Really and why would you do this? Knowing that I will take advantage of it,' he didn't understand his game plan.

Kane meanwhile got Bob in a choke hold, Bob began hitting his plate armour to try to escape but only damaging himself, Kane laughing in his ear so instead he reached into his pocket and pulled out a knife and stabbed his jaw with it but Kane just pulled his head back in time only getting a tiny slice on his chin but it did not draw blood, or any signs of a scratch or mark.

The slice instead had appeared on Abel's chin, the exact same injury by the same knife. Carly saw this and looked to Kane getting a stab in his shoulder only having the wound appeared on Abel instead. *Oh my God,* she said to herself realising what this meant was that the only weakness they had was each other.

Which means I can't win unless Bob hurts Kane, Wolfe said to himself. 'If one dies then the other will be invincible.'

Abel nodded. 'It all depends on which one of the lesser evils you wanna face last, both of us are quite deadly to be left alone anyway,' he said to him getting ready to attack again, 'Now while you cannot harm me I can harm you,' he thrusted forward sending more slices at Wolfe who went back to dodging and moving back.

Carly stood between the two battles, on one side was Wolfe vs Abel while the other was Bob vs Kane. Both knights were dodging their attacks and fighting back faster making it hard for both men to completely dodge in time. She took a deep breath, focusing on her talent. She opened her eyes, glowing white and bright.

She sensed insects, bugs and other creepy crawlies nearby and all around her and far. She held out her hands and spread out her palms to summon the creatures to her aid.

Bob got himself in a chokehold, Kane pressing his arm over his throat choking the air out of him, he punched and kicked but he wouldn't let go, Bob started seeing darkness creeping into his vision. Kane mouthed some words but he did not hear for he was on the brink of passing out. Kane held up his knuckles planning to pummel his skull in to finish him off when suddenly in the corner of his vision, Bob spotted a spider.

Not just any spider, it was the Funnel-Web spider one of Australia's deadliest insects. If you ever got bit by one of these, you must reach the hospital immediately otherwise the venom will kill you quickly making them one of the deadliest spiders in the country. He watched it crawl along his neck finding a vein. Among the veins bulging out, the spider gave one great big bite to one of those. He did not feel the sharp pinch on his neck but his brother did.

Abel screamed out in pain. Kane looked back at his brother clutching his neck in agony, his sword discarded by his feet and Wolfe standing afar with a confused look, watching him spurt out blood, 'Brother!' he called out but was stopped suddenly by something wrapping around his foot making him trip backwards. He looked down to see a snake wrapping around his leg.

The Eastern Brown Snake another one of Australia's venomous creatures. It wraps around its prey then bites them with its venomous fangs so the prey could become paralysed, easy for eating whole. Abel yelled louder and fell back now frozen on the spot.

Kane got to his feet and ran towards him but he soon spotted an insect flying around his brother. Looking closer he saw a wasp along with its other friends swarming onto Abel stinging him with their stingers sending venom into his veins, well, now into Kane's veins.

He screamed falling onto the ground at arm's length to Abel. Both knights were now dying by the venoms inside them. Since they both got bit roughly at the same time, they will die at the same time, thus no immortal guardian to fight afterwards.

Three sets of footsteps came towards them, the knights looked up to see Wolfe, Bob and Carly standing over them.

'Are they dying?' asked Bob.

Carly nodded, 'They were the only insects I could summon, trust me I did not wanna do it but I did not have a choice,' she looked at him feeling guilty, 'They were going to kill you guys I could not just stand by and watch.'

'Don't worry Carly you did not have a choice,' Wolfe assured her, 'In wars you make a life or death choice whether it's your life or your opponents.'

The knights' anger flared behind their eyes, refusing to let them win the brothers reached out to each other grasping each other's fingers.

Bob turned towards the door, 'We should get going, who knows how much time we wasted already.'

'With that spell on the tower it would be impossible to climb,' Wolfe told them, 'Guess we got no choice but to take the stairs.'

The brothers held hands emitting a glow bright as the sun and getting the attention of the trio making them turn and watch. The knights formed into two orbs of light merging together and growing bigger and bigger and bigger sprouting four arms out of the sides. The right side wielded two swords while the left wielded two axes. The glow faded showing the two heads of the brothers on the shoulders now looking the exact same. Long black hair covered their faces and reached down their chins hiding the same scowl and glared under his or their bangs.

Kane and Abel had become one.

With a loud roar, they swung the axes in the air sending a shockwave towards them sending them flying backwards from the huge gust of wind. The trio hit the car and knocked it over, Bob impacted the ceiling while Wolfe and Carly hit the two ends.

'Great they fused now what?' Bob yelled leaning up on his arm and poking his head from beside the car.

Carly got on her knees, sure she's glad she did not kill them but right now she kinda wished she did.

Wolfe stood up, charging up his fists with his talent. 'We get past them and into that door,' he told them stepping forward towards the knights. The knights chuckled and walked up towards him as well.

'I am Taskmaster Wolfe, talent user of the London Hub, you two are endangering the mortals of this world,' he stopped right in front of them.

Kane and Abel laughed. 'You cannot stop us now. mortal, we have joined together so there is no weakness to exploit or any damage your pathetic talent will do to us,' they said speaking with two voices mashed together.

'It is my job to protect the mortal world,' Wolfe said putting one foot forward. Bob and Carly watched from the car while, he used all his power and charged it into his right fist getting ready to punch them with everything he had left.

'Stand down or die.'

Wolfe punched the knights sending a shockwave powerful enough to knock down a building right into the one spot on their torso. But it did nothing only made a dark mark on their armour. Wolfe dropped his hand, the realisation hitting him that there was nothing he could do now.

With a mighty laugh Kane and Abel plunged a sword right into his chest.

Chapter 14

Mr Red had entered the top of the tower.

The wind howled around him while he prepared the doorway into his brother's prison. He held the rock out which had begun to glow, then it floated from his hand into a giant donut shaped rock at the edge of the tower.

The rock began to morph inward and outward growing into a spinal shape and finally into a form of a flower sprouting magic vines that attached to the edges of the hole until it made a web that glowed bright like the stars in the sky. Soon, the stars also went out until the only light left is the key, Mr Red then began the ritual.

Taking his glasses off his eyes, he began looking dead ahead through the key. 'The mortals think they can hide you from me,' he said, 'But mortals don't have an access to the high levels like we do.'

Chanting the incantation spell the donut began to glow as well making the top of the tower bright. The web shot out a beam from its centre into the sky hitting a star, then the star opened up wider until it is large enough for a person to walk through. The light then made a bridge connecting the tower to the door solid enough to walk on with no worry of falling through, well as along as you don't lose your balance. Mr Red stood up and began walking on the bright road. He walked along it over the air away from the top of the tower and towards the door stepping into a dark black void.

There was nothing here, no light, no air, no sight and no magic. Anyone who walked in here will be permanently blinded without any chance of seeing the way out. This was the dark space between dimensions that the taskmasters used as a perfect prison.

But Mr Red was not like any other, he was a guardian with no eyes to blind and his magic gave him all the air he needed so he walked along the white road towards the cube suspended in nothingness, 'So, this is where they're keeping you,' he said touching the side with his fingers. The Cube was smooth but more than that it felt like there was nothing there, even when he could see it and touch it.

Mr Red knew the magic that was used for this; it was ancient magic that was far older than the magic of the guardians. But that meant its weakness was as simple. It was here in the void where the rules of physics didn't apply. Any force or contact with anything outside the void could prove effective on its defence. Putting his face towards the cube, he gave one simple blow which made the Cube crack.

It shattered like a fragile glass of a window top to bottom raining down into the darkness, leaving a person standing in the middle. This man was clothed in white robes with a single yellow scarf floating around him, he opened his bright blue eyes to see his brother standing beyond him, opening his mouth to say…

'Dear God I need the toilet!' he yelled in pain.

Mr Red sighed, figured since he had been there for thirty years, 'You can go when we leave brother,' he said.

The first guardian chuckled, 'Ah Mr Red! How have you been? Er, how long have I been here?' he asked walking on the air towards him.

'Well, our brothers are driving me up the wall but that doesn't matter right now,' he told him, 'Now is the time for us to rid our planet of the mortals.'

The First placed his hand on his chin, 'I see, what about that young mortal that got me imprisoned? Surely, he wouldn't let me walk out of here, scot free,' he said, 'What was his name again? Wort or Worm…'

'Wolfe,' Mr Red said.

'Ah Yes! Interesting mortal, isn't he?' he chuckled.

'He is being dealt with as we speak, he and his apprentice are prophesised to defeat us,' he told him of the prophecy and how the guardians will fall by a taskmaster and his apprentice. The First listened and contemplated this.

'You and your prophesies, surely they could be wrong this time like that time you prophesised that Cows will take over

Greenland and we spent the whole year pleasing them in very questionable ways,' he said laughing a bit at that memory.

But Mr Red just groaned. 'That was different,' he said. 'This time they killed three of our brothers,' he told him, 'Wolfe and Carly will be dead by morning I can assure you that.'

The First nodded walking past him towards the door. 'Let's leave this place, you understand. I wanna see the sky again,' he said walking out through the door.

Mr Red followed him into the bright road. 'I thought you might be a little bit mad,' he asked, 'Seeing these mortals are afraid of our power and tried to destroy us.'

The First said nothing, only looking ahead at the tower when a scream rang out from the ground beneath them. The two guardians looked down to see their brother or brothers since they did that weird morph thing, impaling Wolfe with their sword.

'Well, I guess Wolfe won't be a problem anymore,' The First said.

Mr Red smiled, 'We have beaten the prophecy, without him, his apprentice will die easily,' his smile got wider, 'Finally this world will be ours.'

The First looked closer, 'I say who is that chap there on the ground with them?'

Mr Red shrugged, 'Just some prisoner they picked up he is no threat,' he told him.

The First looked back and continued crossing into the tower, hoping he could find the toilets soon.

Chapter 15

Carly screamed out his name feeling her chest hollowed out while Wolfe fell to the ground getting the sword pulled from his chest. Kane and Abel laughed in victory.

She ran to him and knelt by his side, blinking back tears while she tried to stop the bleeding refusing to lose another family. Kane and Abel took this moment to strike her while she was distraught but Bob sent a smoke bomb into his face making them falter and fall back rubbing their eyes with two hands of the right side.

Blood started pouring onto her hands while she begged Wolfe to stay alive. 'Please Wolfe, hang in there we can heal you,' she told him, her tears falling onto his tattered shirt. Bob kneeled beside her putting a hand on her shoulder.

'Carly,' he began but she did not listen.

Wolfe coughed, 'Carly listen…' he said, putting a hand to her face so she can face him, 'It's OK, my young apprentice, I'm afraid my journey ends here.'

'Don't say that,' sobbed Carly.

'Listen to me,' he said firmly this time, Carly sniffed and she listened, 'You will be a powerful Taskmaster one day, I know you can do it but you need to have hope and believe in yourself, the only thing holding you back is your doubt,' he told her, 'Don't let it control you, you are the only one who can rise higher than anyone.'

'But for that you need a taskmaster to guide you and I can think of no one better than Bob,' now it was Bob's turn to look at him. Wolfe faced him now. 'Promise me, you will take care of her,' he asked holding out his hand to him, 'Teach her your courage, your optimism, I know she will inherit it from you,' he said chuckling.

'But I don't want to,' Bob said.

'I'm dying here you don't have a choice mate,' Wolfe chuckled, 'Promise me,' he held his hand higher now. Carly could see the sorrow on Bob's face.

So he took his hand and instantly Wolfe's Electricity began zapping around them sending charges through Bob, making him go wide eyed as the talent surged into his body. Carly watched all the talent Wolfe had left surged into him. Bob stood back having the electricity charging around him now, holding up his hand to feel the power running inside it.

'I have given you my talent,' Wolfe told him coughing out more blood, 'It is an ancient technique to give a taskmaster a second talent, but it has never been tried since the result usually ends with someone blowing up.'

'Wait what?!'

'From this day forward, you are now the Taskmaster Bob, mentor of Carly and taskmaster of the Australian Hub.'

'Yeah, yeah what was that part about blowing up?'

'Wolfe…' Carly looked back at him, seeing him make that stupid grin.

Kane and Abel eyes were now better, 'We will make you pay for that!' leaping forward he held both his axes and swords for one final slash at the trio. 'Time for all of you to DIE!' he roared.

Bob suddenly stepped in front of his path sending an electric charged kick straight into his side. Kane and Abel roared in pain flying into the door of the tower, it wasn't enough to break it down. Kane and Abel just got angrier standing up and held onto their weapons tighter now.

'Fight the good fight,' Wolfe said to her before closing his eyes for the final time.

'Fine, I promise you old man,' Bob said, 'Sheesh, twist my neck, why don't you?'

The talent ran through his leg, Carly had never heard of someone with two talents but right now Bob got both his and Wolfe's. Kane/Abel took a step forward while Bob casually walked towards him or them? Ah who cares.

'So, what if he gave you a useless power up, it won't save you mortal,' they said together, 'I'll slice you up then that girl is next.'

Bob stopped right in front of him now. 'I am Taskmaster Bob,' he started with a grin, copying what Wolfe said earlier, 'Of

119

the Australian Hub,' Kane and Abel swung the sword and axe down upon him planning to slice him up like a tomato but Bob charged up electricity and swung both arms into the oncoming weapons breaking their blades into two, 'You two are endangering the mortals of this world and murdered my friend Wolfe,' he finally looked up at him showing the fury in his eyes. Kane and Abel took a step back.

'Stand down or die.'

A fist struck their face then to the abdomen, then to the chest, arm, neck and anything that he could hit. Bob punched furiously into a barrage of furious punches. With the talent that Wolfe gave him Bob looked like he had fifty arms punching Kane and Abel within a second each. All pounding him fast and relentless until his armour started to crack and break. Kane and Abel did not have any time to defend or to counterattack each time they tried, they were met with more punches. Bob was yelling with all his might while the electricity surged around his hands.

With one mighty roar Bob sent one final punch into their jaws and sent them flying into the door, crashing right through and leaving a giant hole for them to enter.

Upon impact Kane and Abel split back into the two knights, Abel fell by the new entrance while Kane hit the ground many times before reaching the stairs. Both were unable to move or get up from that last attack.

With a deep breath, Bob stopped the electricity flowing into his hands. He walked back to Carly still kneeling by Wolfe's side. She was now his responsibility and like it or not he would honour Wolfe's final request.

Carly wiped away her tears and getting to her feet. 'So you're my new mentor,' she said.

'Looks like it,' Bob replied in that tone of his.

'Even though you have no idea about this side of the world, or how talent works or anything for that matter,' she continued giving a small smile for a bit, 'But if you get clueless maybe I can give you some advice for a change.'

Bob folded his arms. 'OK, maybe Wolfe wanted to mess with me for one last time,' he said, 'Either way, I guess, you're stuck with me now, or until I blow up.'

'Yeah only Wolfe would do that,' she said looking at her former mentor lying peacefully, 'Either way I'm glad it would be you,' she said silently looking back down.

'We'll give him a proper burial after we finish this,' he said looking up at the bright road hanging over the tower, ''Cause it looks like we're too late.'

'Oh, give me a break,' said Carly giving off a moan, 'Does this mean we have to fight The First now?'

'Yep, hope you're ready kid, 'cause unlike Wolfe I am not saving your skin,' Bob turned towards the door. Carly stuck out her tongue at him then followed both entering the huge hole where the guardians they defeated lay. Abel was on his knees holding what's left of his broken sword.

'You will not pass,' he said coldly, blood covered half his face. 'On the honour of my brothers, you will not pass as long as I draw breath,' he yelled getting to his feet now and holding his sword in a battle stance.

'Give me a break,' Bob said not stopping as he came towards Abel who swung his sword up high and gave out a battle cry but Bob ignored him and walked past. Carly was still back at the entrance surprised as hell that he did not even give a second look, even Abel stood shocked as well.

He put down his sword and turned towards his back. Carly ran forward fearing he will attack while his back was turned but Abel just put his sword down on the ground. 'Why did you not kill us?!' he demanded.

That's when he stops still having his back turned. 'What good will that do,' he just said.

'I killed your friend and was going to kill the girl, don't you want some sort of vengeance?' he asked, 'Aren't you angry?' he thought he understood the minds of mortals, knowing they were selfish, arrogant and dangerous. But for some strange reason this mortal was a mystery to him, why did he kill his brothers but spared him and his twin.

'It won't bring him back,' he said finally, 'Anger and revenge are a pointless cause that will only make me feel twice as bad and insult the memory of my friend,' he turned to face him, 'I'm not a killer like you or your kind. If you want to keep killing innocent people, that's your business. I'll be there to knock you down anytime.'

Abel could not believe his ears. He thought that he was just like the rest but this mortal was different.

Carly jogged a bit to catch up to Bob, sure if it was up to her she would have left these two dead in a ditch somewhere but Wolfe's legacy and Bob's words burnt within her mind so well that she didn't want to soil his memory as well. But then a movement caught the corner of her eye. She looked towards the walls, this place was one giant circle with the stairs at the end across from the where the door used to be.

But the shadows moved all around them, Bob saw it too. They both stood back to back, Bob readying his hands with electricity while Carly held up her fists. A figure jumped out right at them, a shrivelled-up corpse with no skin covering his jaws and dressed in an ancient knight outfit came right at Carly. Bob turned and punched the Corpse's jaw right off his skull. Then he kicked him back into the shadows where more of them came jumping out all wielding different weapons and shields. Swords, axes, mallets and sickles they came right at the two mortals.

Bob hit two of them; Carly kicked one then sent a sweeping kick to another. The corpses surrounded them now and came at them one by one, soon two by two then they all figured to attack them at the same time, damn these clever pricks.

They all swarmed over them; Carly got her hair pulled along with her arms and leg. Bob was getting piled on by hundreds of them all holding him down. Carly head butted the one behind her then she kicked the ones pulling her legs, punching and scratching her way out but there were too many. Hearing Bob call out she turned and ducked the fire that barely missed her, seeing Bob holding an electric charged flamethrower in his hands, burning all the corpses that easily caught on fire. 'Hey you nearly burned me you jerk!' she yelled towards him sending jabs into more corpses.

'I told ya to, duck!' he yelled back running out of ammo so he used the gun as a bat and swung at more corpses coming right at him. Breaking more skulls and sending them flying, Carly punched more skulls in but they kept coming, dodging some she jumped and rolled across the floor kicking and pounding until she got on her feet. Huffing now she stood back against the wall while the Corpses came towards her from every angle. She heard growling from above so she looked up to see more crawling on the walls. 'Give me a break,' she said punching those who come close.

Bob was too busy hitting his ones with the gun while more seem to keep coming, they surrounded them yet again. Carly punched, kicked and bit, yes, she was desperate, give her a break, while a gleam of light appeared in the middle.

Abel held his sword high; despite it being broken he did not care. He swung it around sending a gust of wind that cut all the corpses in half, luckily it did not cut them in half as well. Carly held a head before she chucked it away and walked over the bodies towards the two guardians getting up, Kane holding his axe and gave her a glare, and a growl.

'Thanks,' Bob said coming towards them.

'You have spared our lives, for that honour we will forever be in your debt,' Abel told him sheathing his sword, 'Mr Red is at the top and no doubt already has our brother with him.'

'Yeah, I figured,' Bob said taking a glance up. 'So you gonna let us fight them?' he asked turning back to them.

Abel shook his head. 'I have a feeling that Mr Red had lied to us, so I will ask you to let him explain himself but we will not let you hurt our older brother he had nothing to do with this,' he told him.

'We won't as long as he doesn't give us a reason to,' Bob said, 'As for Mr Red, dumb name by the way, I have a feeling that he won't share your loyalty.'

'He can be very rash but we shall deal with our brother.'

'We got one hell of a fight up there, didn't we?' he then started to climb the stairs and looked back at them, 'So you're coming?'

Carly nodded and followed along with one of the knights following behind, Kane grunted but he said nothing while Abel walked beside them.

Carly reached up to Bob. 'You sure we should let them come? They did try to kill us after all,' she asked feeling very uncomfortable with them.

'You have spared our lives, if you killed our brothers like we were told then you should've killed us,' Abel explained walking next to her now, Carly could feel Kane's breath on her neck behind her, 'So our brother will explain the truth to us.'

'Did he tell you?'

Abel nodded. 'He told us you killed Drybon, Mozart and Mickle, in our anger we acted too hastily,' he admitted, 'Now seeing the honour of your comrade here, I have doubts about our brother's claim, therefore he will explain himself or meet my sword.'

Half a sword, Carly thought.

'I still wanna rip your guts out,' Kane said, 'But I trust Abel and Mr Red is a prick.' he adjusted his axe on his shoulder.

'What is his magic?' asked Bob not looking at the back, 'If things go south then we need to know what we're up against.'

Abel sighed, 'We do not know, he is the oldest out of all of us and in all that time he never takes his glasses off,' he put a finger to his chin, contemplating in his head, 'In fact, I believe his magic has to do with his eyes.'

'So, all we gotta do is not look into his eyes?' Carly said.

'Doesn't matter if we look or not, I believe he just has to look at you then you will be dead, we have never actually seen it in action,' Abel told her.

'Great, so how do we make him not look at us?' she turned to Bob. 'I don't suppose you have any ideas?' she asked him but of course he doesn't say, 'Ah, of course we'll silence him to death.'

'You are annoying,' Kane said to her.

'I agree,' Bob said.

'Oh, now you answer!' Carly yelled.

Abel just chuckled, 'Ah this must be what mortals do in the face of death, mock each other.'

Carly groaned; great she's going to die with people she hates not the way she wanted to go.

They moved through more flights of stairs soon reaching a door at the end. Bob stood in front of it, Carly and Abel behind him and Kane at the back, all ready for the fight that's about to begin. Bob put his hand on the door and pushed it open, walking into the room inside.

They entered into a nice furnished room, red carpet on the ground while the walls were lined with lights, lighting the room, the stairs to the top were behind the huge king-sized door across from them. A figure stood guarding it, a man wearing a long black coat, his hair deep red like blood and wearing deep black sunglasses. He stood calmly watching Bob and his crew walked in.

'Is this Mr Red?' Bob asked.

Abel nodded, 'That's him,' he pointed then walking past him to stand in the centre of the room facing him. 'Brother! Tell me the truth of our brother's demise,' he demanded.

Mr Red clenched his teeth, 'You demand me? You have betrayed the guardians by siding with these mortals,' he reached up to his glasses and grabbed the rim, 'You were supposed to kill them, but not only have you been beaten but you led them to your brother,' he took them off showing his closed eyes.

Abel yelled out, 'You told us, he killed them but why did he spare our lives?' he grabbed the hilt of his sword, 'You were the last one to see them alive so tell me did you kill your own brethren?'

Mr Red sighed, 'You ungrateful pigs, we own this planet more than the mortals but every step we take to achieve my goal of a perfect world, my brothers seem to mess it up along the way.'

Abel pulled out his sword. 'So now I see, it was you wasn't it,' he said, 'You killed them!'

Kane growled clenching his axe, 'You LIED to us!'

His eyes were closed, Abel came charging at him holding the hilt of his sword behind him as he plans to slice him. 'How dare you betray US!' he yelled swinging it over himself for a deadly blow.

But he opened his eyes.

He stared down Abel who went frozen in place. Abel looked directly at them sweating from the top of his head he fell to his knees, dropping his sword beside him. Carly could not understand what was happening, she tried to look at his eyes but her vision was covered by a hand, 'Don't,' Bob's voice said to her, 'You shouldn't look at his eyes.'

'What's happening?' she asked looking up at him but she could see that Bob was too busy looking at Abel watching the effect of the magic.

Abel was screaming, inside his mind, he was seeing a tall black and red figure forming Anubis, God of Death of the Egyptian era. He had begun the weighing of the heart, a tradition among ancient Egypt where the dead will be judged by the scales. The scales had Abel's heart on one side with a feather on the other. They both rose and were lowered until finally his heart hit the ground with the feather high in the air.

Having been judged Abel's eyes began smoking, his soul burning within him. Anubis roared a dark hollow sound and began to burn bright red with flames filling up his vision. Abel screamed a high pitch screech from his final breath until finally he hit the ground; his eyes are now burning craters.

Carly began to shake; he did not even do anything, just looked at the guy and now suddenly his eyes burnt up. Kane roared with fury and charged at him with his axe clenched in his hands, but it was too late. Mr Red took one look at him for him to stop, he soon began screaming and burning just like his brother before him. He fell to the ground now a lifeless corpse.

'My magic can kill even an immortal, they never stood a chance,' he turned to Bob and Carly with his eyes closed but ready to open them, 'Now mortals, do you think you can beat me?'

Bob stepped forward with no hesitation and gave him one of his glares, 'I don't think, I know.'

Chapter 16

Mr Red's laugh echoed around the room.

Carly stood her ground; she will not let him intimidate her. Bob showed no fear, he could die within a look from this guardian but he did not care.

Mr Red's laughter quieted down. 'Oh that is quite funny,' he said, 'You have guts mortal thinking you can beat my magic,' he shook his head, 'My eyes can see the truth, they can judge you for all your wrongdoings, I have the power to judge you for who you really are,' he slowly opened his eyes towards him, 'You mortals call yourself noble but deep down you all are selfish and pure evil,' his eyes were now fully opened, 'Allow me prisoner to judge you for whom you really…'

His eyes began burning after being sprayed by the pepper spray in Bob's hand.

Mr Red screamed and rubbed his eyes while tears ran down his face, 'I'm sorry what were you saying,' Bob said throwing the spray away and held up his hand to his ear, 'I can't hear over you screaming like a little girl.'

Mr Red could not see he had been blinded by a simple spray. Bob took this chance to start punching him relentlessly, one punch to the face then the body and over again. Carly cheered him on, while the guardian is unable to see the punches coming and continue being pounded like a punching bag. He sent out a gust of wind towards Bob which sent him back so he could take a few steps away as well to catch his bearings. Carly then came running to him and sent a kick to his back, 'Forgot about me, did you?' she said with such confidence.

'ENOUGH!' he slammed the ground, cracking it and sending a shockwave that hit both of them. They impacted the walls and fell down but Bob already got back on his feet again facing Mr Red, who turned to his direction and opened his eyes towards him, 'I will not be humiliated by MORTALS!' He came closer, Bob tried to look away but it was too late for now he sees Anubis for his own judgment of the heart.

Carly got to her feet and looked towards them. 'Bob!' she yelled running forward refusing to lose another person. She jumped onto the guardians back and placed her hands around his eyes, 'Guess who!' she yelled out wrapping her legs around him to hold on tight.

'Get off me you little vermin!' he yelled grabbing her hands trying to pull them off and also attempting to shake her off. Carly held on for dear life refusing to let go. Bob shook the vision out of his head and went to help her, sending more punches into him. Mr Red's yells were cut short by one punch to the jaw splattering blood on to Bob's face.

'Get off Carly,' he told her.

Carly listened and jumped off, standing way back while Mr Red stared angrily at Bob, and got another spray to the eyes, 'GODDAMMIT!' he screamed rubbing his eyes again.

'Yeah, we mortals can be evil,' Bob said getting his attention, 'There are mortals who kill innocent people, mortals who manipulate others for money and power, hell there are some who just like to watch everything burn,' he pointed a finger to him. Mr Red facing him now with his eyes closed, 'But there are mortals who help people; they protect the weak and defenceless from people like you who use power to prey on them.'

The two men stood facing each other now. 'What right do you have to judge us for our sins?' Bob said clenching his fists now, summoning the electricity to charge them up, 'You who killed your own brothers for your obsession, you have become the evil you speak of.'

'Don't compare me to you,' he growled, 'I am a higher being than you.'

'And that gives you the right?'

'That gives me all the right!' he yelled back, 'I will cleanse this world of the mortals, so we sorcerers could finally live in peace! For us to use our magic freely and out in the open as much as we want! I am doing this for them!'

'You did this for yourself.'

He opened his eyes wide to Bob, 'Justice belongs to us! I will reclaim our right on this planet!' Bob looked directly into his eye's electricity charging faster around his hands now, 'With the power of my brother, I will bring us all to our rightful place above you all!'

'BOB!' Carly yelled to him running to help him but Mr Red released an aura, so powerful, it begun creating a whirlwind around him and Bob. She couldn't go closer or use her talent to save him making her powerless.

But Bob stood strong against the wind, facing down his enemy with no sign of fear or regret. 'If that is what you believe,' he said firmly, 'Then it's your turn to be judged.'

Bob put on the sunglasses, Mr Red recognised those and felt around his pockets but could not find his glasses anywhere, how did he take them?! He must have charged his hands fast enough to pickpocket him in that struggle with the girl. His glasses were black and void enough to create a reflection in the lens making him look into his own eyes!

Soon he was looking at Anubis, holding the scales right in front of him. 'NO!' he screamed trying desperately to close his eyes but he could not, for his heart was already on the plate, 'I WILL NOT BE JUDGED!' but the weighing had begun. Seeing the feather rising to the top he did the unthinkable, pulling out two small knives from his pockets and dug them right into his own eye sockets.

Blood burst forth from them; Bob had to step back from the shock of seeing him do that to himself. 'Jesus,' he whispered seeing blood pour out of his eyes.

Mr Red yelled in rage, the black holes that are now his eyes dripped with blood. He gritted his teeth while he reclaimed his composure. 'I will not let you win,' he told Bob growling in his voice.

Bob looked closer at him. Carly stood on the sides watching this fight with all of her attention, marvelling at how intense this is. Bob took a step forward expecting a reaction from the guardian but he did not seem to notice.

'It's over,' Bob told him, 'You can't see a damn thing, plus your magic relies on your eyesight,' he came even closer, 'Without that you are just another mortal like the rest of us.'

He clenched his fist. 'No, it is not over,' he said.

The air around him began to turn, Carly could feel her hair blowing against her and covering her eyes. She moved them out of the way so she could see the whirlwind blowing around Mr Red. Bob began to be blown away but he stood hard on the ground, the wind had begun scratching him now with sharp breezes.

He was moving the air so fast that they were like tiny swords flying and cutting at Bob everywhere with no way to block or fight back. Bob tried getting closer to him, but the wind was so harsh it pushed him away, not to mention it sent more cuts on his skin. Carly wanted to help but the wind stopped her from coming closer as well, the only reason Bob was that close was because of Wolfe's talent helping him move, otherwise, he would've been blown back into the wall and be a sitting duck for Mr Red.

The cuts from the wind had become more intense and with more speed around them. Mr Red could not see a single thing but he could still feel the aura of his opponent near him trying to get through the wind but he made sure it would be impossible even with his talent. 'Give it up, mortal!' he called out to him, 'You were doomed the minute you decided to get in our way.'

The winds burst harder making a small hurricane around them, Carly screamed out Bob's name, but her voice was muffled by the sounds of the whirlwinds. Bob kept getting more cuts, his top shredding to pieces along with his skin, he blocked himself with his arms now trying in vain to cover his face while his arms take the most damage.

The guardian held his hands up high at that moment. Carly was then blown back against the wall screaming as the wind cut into her now. The hurricane wasn't like anything she had ever seen, it's now even worse than hurricane Irene or something more deadly! Bob started walking closer, taking big steps through the wind while Mr Red makes the wind swirl around with more force, 'You can't win now, mortal! The prophecy predicted that a taskmaster and his apprentice will stop the guardians, and you are no Taskmaster.'

Bob took one look at him, 'Don't need to be one to pound your head into the wall,' he just said pulling out a sledgehammer out of what's left of his sleeve and flung it away into the hurricane. Then he dropped to the ground and covered his head.

Carly managed to turn her head to see a sledgehammer speeding just past her face and miss her nose by inches that she could have given it a kiss.

Mr Red laughed. 'I feel something heavy in the winds, I bet it was a last-minute weapon of yours,' he laughed harder, 'Too bad my wind blew it out of your hands.'

'If you could see, you would have noticed that I chucked it on purpose,' Bob said from the ground.

In that moment, the sledgehammer was tossed around in that much speed that the impact into Mr Red's skull was even more serious. The metal burst right into his skull that it stuck there in its hole it made. The impact knocked him from his feet and sent him flying into his own hurricane. Mr Red screamed, the winds dying down now since he lost focus having his head dented on the top once the hammer flown off. Both the hammer and Mr Red fell face first on the ground, forming a pool of his blood.

The winds had now stopped, sending silence into the room. Bob stood up and ignored Carly walking up and pounding his injured arm repeatedly. 'You big dumb jerk that hammer nearly bashed my face in have you thought of that?!' she yelled up continuing her punches.

'I have actually,' he said.

'OH MY GOD!'

She finally stopped right when Bob walked towards the guardian, making a note to have a talk with him later while following him. Looking down at him she could not help but feel a sense of accomplishment; they won, the bad guy was down and they saved the world. But she felt like the fight wasn't over yet.

A door opened up from the side, a man walked out and threw away a newspaper. 'Finally, a proper toilet,' he said stopping in his tracks.

They both watched him with caution. This man had long blonde hair flowing around him along with his scarf, hell she could not tell which one was the scarf and which one was the hair. 'It's the first brother,' she whispered.

'Tarous.'

Tarous looked up at them and smiled but soon his gaze fell to his brother on the ground, 'Oh dear, it seems we got ourselves a problem.'

Chapter 17

Bob and Carly stood with their guard up keeping their eyes on the first guardian who walked to his injured brother on the floor, half dead from the looks of it. Tarous stood over him while he shakily reaches for him.

'Brother, you must use your power now,' he said up to him getting to his knees now like he is begging, 'Use your magic to wipe all mortals off the planet, so we sorcerers can live with peace!'

'He can do that?' Bob asked Carly.

'Yeah, his magic is reality itself, he can wipe out all the mortals if he feels like it, that must be why Wolfe had him locked up, 'cause he was afraid that this would happen,' she explained, 'If he uses that spell you, me and everyone who isn't magic will get wiped out.'

'This is something I would've preferred to know yesterday you damn old man,' mumbled Bob considering if he would go to Wolfe's funeral now. He then turned his attention back to Tarous who looked back at them.

He cracked his head side to side, flexing his fingers and adjusting his shoulder. Bob and Carly knew they must do something about him otherwise they came all this way for nothing. Carly charged at him but was suddenly pulled back by Bob holding the top of her shirt. 'Wait,' he said.

Wait? For what? Carly thought, turning back to him seeing the focus on his face and have not taken his eyes off the guardian. She turned back to see Mr Red on his feet, well, barely since he was short of breath which was making him gasp and wheeze.

'Do it,' he said, 'Do it for all of us who have suffered at their hands, all the countless sorcerers who are too afraid to use their gifts, do it for us brother...'

'Nah, I don't want to.'

Immediately Carly and Mr Red dropped their jaws. 'WHAT?!' they both yelled.

'What do you mean you don't want to?' Mr Red demanded grabbing his robes for him to face him but Tarous just smiled, not taking his gaze off Bob.

''Cause if all mortals were to die then who would make those delicious pizza. Is Pizza Hut still around by the way?'

'THAT'S YOUR REASON?!'

'Think of it brother,' begun Tarous turning to him, 'Mortals may not be powerful and they may be weak and useless not to mention how cowardly they can be…'

'Standing over here you know,' Carly said under her breath.

'But they have courage, and mostly they made all these cool inventions, have you heard of a game called Pokémon Go? I discovered it on a phone, I found in the toilet apparently you catch these mythical beings isn't that wonderful!' he beamed.

'How do you know about that?' Bob yelled out to him,

'I could still watch the world from my cell, Mr Stewart,' Tarous said to him, 'I have witnessed what mortals went through, tsunamis, earthquakes, fires, each trial you all face and overcome together, that is what makes you mortals so different from us. Your commitment to doing the right thing even when you aren't realising what you are doing.'

'But they locked you up for years!' Mr Red growled.

'Eh, I would've done the same thing,' he admitted, 'I am pretty powerful so of course they wanna lock me up, how do you think they caught me in the first place.'

'You let them catch you!'

'Yep, even gave them the idea of the cell too, pretty cool eh?'

'Huh, I always wondered why he did not put up a fight,' Carly said remembering Wolfe telling her about the capture.

'Yeah, I need to see that file he made when we get back,' Bob sighed rubbing his forehead, 'What a waste of time.'

'But why would you do this? Let these mortals capture and cage you like an animal?' Mr Red asked him, his whole world and his plans were crashing down around him.

'Well, the cell was nice just needed a real toilet, but mostly I just wanted to get away from you guys,' he admitted, 'You all are way too annoying and whiny, always finding new ways to complain about mortals,' If this was a cartoon, Mr Red's jaw would have hit the ground, or he would've fallen on his back at the revelations he was hearing. Tarous began walking away from him. 'Yeah, I've been watching you on your journey, Mr Stewart, or may I call you Bob?' he asked holding out his hand for a handshake.

Bob chuckled, no doubt enjoying seeing Mr Red like this. He grabbed his hand and shook. 'Well, it has been a wild ride, two of my friends died because of this whole mess you know that,' he added with a glare.

'Yes, you have my apologies,' Tarous said letting go, 'I know what you two went through, I can never make up for but how about I start by buying you a beer?'

'It's a start.'

This had to be the weirdest thing Carly had ever witnessed; the big bad is actually a big good and now he is going to buy Bob a beer and not destroy the world. Maybe this was all a dream, although she wasn't complaining about the world not ending so she could call this one a win.

But Mr Red wasn't done just yet. He was never going to rely on his brother in the first place, 'cause he had a hidden agenda of his own. He grabbed his brother's shoulder emitting a strange magical current flowing from his hand and wrapping around Tarous. With wide eyes he looked back at him, 'Brother please,' he said knowing what is about to happen.

Bob and Carly stood back; they recognised the current as the same thing that happen with Wolfe and Bob earlier when he transferred his talent but this one was different. They tried to save him but the magic's power was keeping them back while Mr Red began the incantation, the magic flowing back into his hand and powering his body but the magic was dragging Tarous's life essence as well. Tarous screamed and fell to his knees while Mr Red stood over him. 'You...' he managed to say, 'All this time you planned for this.'

'I did not want to, I thought you would see things more clearly once I set you free,' Mr Red said, 'But you are just as naïve as ever.'

'This magic is uncontrollable, you will never be able to handle it,' Tarous fell to his hands his skin getting lighter, his hair falling out as he seemed to be aging rapidly like the thousands of years he was alive are catching up to him.

'What is he doing?' Carly called out.

'He is taking my magic,' Tarous said.

She gulped knowing this was really bad, Mr Red hated all mortals and would not hesitate a second to erase them all, 'We gotta do something!' she yelled turning to Bob.

Bob nodded, using his talent he grabbed Carly and swung her on his back. She held on tight while Bob began walking towards them.

'I don't think so!' Mr Red yelled blowing them across the room; Bob fell back on Carly against the wall, her injury sending a shock up her spine. Soon, she fell on the ground while Bob remained on his feet.

Tarous fell as well, his body fragile and wrinkled up. Mr Red stood up feeling the magic of The First in him.

Slowly, all the blood began to flow back into his wounds, his bones healing as well as his eyes returning to their glory once again. Now he could see the result of what he did. Tarous dying on the ground, the annoying girl too injured to move and that prisoner standing tall. He tensed his muscles, the magic tearing off his shirt and coat. 'No distractions,' he said.

'You mortals are done,' he told them emitting the enormous power he now had.

He held his hands up high and blew the ceiling to smithereens, the dark night sky hanging over them soon glowed, brighter by Mr Red using his new magic to create a red fierily ring of fire around him. Carly managed to get away just as the ring stopped at her face, the heat burning her more than the country's weather. She sat against the wall watching the magic at play and unable to stop it.

She screamed suddenly feeling her hand burning, grabbing her wrist she looked down to see her hand on fire, 'Bob…' she said with a hollow heart.

'You mortals will all burn,' Mr Red said in the silence, 'Now you will know how we felt.'

Jim drove the truck filled with his finest soldiers. The taskmasters were in their own vehicles following them on the long road towards the tower.

God damn it all, why did we stop at maccas! Now we're so late, Jim said to himself turning the wheel towards the broken giant hole in the entrance, the top of the tower destroyed with a bright light blazing from it. 'Looks like they already started,' he said stopping the engine.

He got out of the truck, everyone getting out when a scream hit his ears. Jim turned to see one soldier caught on fire, 'Damn it Kevin, you're not supposed to be on fire yet!' he yelled to him, 'This is why we don't invite you to these things!'

'Uh sir,' one soldier said coming up to him, 'His talent is not fire, we told you this.'

Jim looked to him then to the burning soldier, then back to him who is now a burning soldier too. He screamed along with the taskmasters, who are on fire too. 'What the bloody hell?' Jim said stepping back.

He felt the heat under his clothes, looking down to see the fire climbing up his legs. 'Oh hell,' he said before bursting into flames. He fell to his knees screaming along with everyone else, forming a giant bonfire before the Tower.

Violet grabbed her desk. The fire had started enveloping her.

Everywhere it's the same, she just knew it.

Her base was filled with people burning, not just there but the whole of Australia. Innocent people being set on fire, well, anyone who wasn't magic was being set on fire. Then the magic spread across the seas into the rest of the world. Leaders burning on TV, athletes burning on the streets. The only people not affected were sorcerers filled with magic.

Some sorcerers tried to help them. Using their magic they tried to put out the flames but it was no use because they couldn't seem to affect the fire no matter how powerful their spells were. It is hard to watch, especially, since some sorcerers had families that did not use magic. They stood there helpless watching them burn before their eyes.

Soon the entire Earth is shown ablaze; in ten minutes all mortals will be left as burnt husks of their former selves, leaving only sorcerers to inherit the Earth.

Violet sat in her chair, her fire ablaze in her office. Taking a cigarette out she put it in her mouth, lucky the fire lit it for her so she could have one final smoke. 'OK, you morons,' she said taking a huff, 'Better not screw this one up.'

Now ablaze, Carly screamed at the top of her lungs. She wanted it to stop but it just hurt so much. She searched around but she could not find Bob anywhere, well, anywhere outside the circle of flames surrounding the guardian.

Looking through the fire she could see him in the centre of it all. He was not on fire like the rest of them.

Mr Red gave a small chuckle, 'You are a smart one, aren't you?' he folded his arms, acting like he already won, 'As long as you're in this ring you won't be set on fire like your kind I gotta admit you have spirit.'

'I'm not done bashing your head in mate,' Bob said.

Mr Red scowled. 'I am so sick of your attitude,' he said putting his arms down, 'Get it through your primitive skull, it's over! With this magic there wasn't a thing you could do to stop me, the only way to stop the extinction is to kill me so it is over!'

'If it's over, then why am I still standing?'

'Because you are a cowardly cockroach who refuses to accept his fate!'

Bob said nothing but just gave his usual glare, but this time there was a rage behind it.

Mr Red sighed, 'No matter, I just have to get you out of the ring, then you can start burning like your friend there, hopefully you will see there is no more hope for your kind.'

Carly gritted her teeth, getting to her knees she does her best to ignore the fire and watch. She had seen hope, when she was beaten down and broken Bob showed her there was always hope in a moment as dark as this. If she was to die like this, then fine, but she would watch her mentor beat this arrogant prick into the ground.

Bob and Mr Red charged at each other, fists raised and ready for round two.

Chapter 18

Eight minutes till the extinction of mortals.

This had become a boxing match. The first punch struck Bob across the jaw, sending him backwards while Mr Red sent more jabs into his torso, finishing with an uppercut that knocked him back to the wall of fire that surrounds them in the ring.

Mr Red grabbed his head and slammed it into the wall burning the side of his face while the guardian tried to force him outside, for if he leaves the ring he will burn like the rest of the mortals of the world. Seeing Carly watching him while being on fire he knows he did not have much time. Placing his hands on the wall, thanks to the electricity of his talent making him touch it, he pushed back and head butted his opponent.

Mr Red stepped back while Bob turned and sent an elbow to his cheek, then sending his own barrage of punches beating him senseless. But he knew that if he wanted the spell to stop, he had to kill him; could he really cross that line just once?

The guardian grabbed his arm, pushing it out of the ring. Bob screamed once it caught on fire, not due to the actual fire but since his arm was outside it is now vulnerable to the spell. Bob kneed his abdomen and punched back; pulling back his arm into the ring which made the fire vanish from it.

Charging his fists, he began his barrage of fists, making twenty punches a second into his face but Mr Red grabbed both hands and smiled, 'It's not like you grew more arms,' he mocked snapping them back.

Bob yelled and fell to his knees, his hands bled and broken. Mr Red used the wind to blow him back into the wall, pushing it until his back had begun going through it. Feeling his back began to catch fire, he clenched his fist and used his talent to push off the wall with his electricity. He got back to his feet and pulled a rock from his pocket, charging it so it can push against the wind he threw it straight at his face.

The rock cracked his jaw, damaging him enough that the wind dropped. Seizing this chance, Bob charged through and tackled him, sending him on the ground and punched him with his broken hands, hurting himself in the process but he was willing to take that sacrifice.

Mr Red just laughed, 'This was your chance to kill me but you're hesitating!' he sent red-hot flames into the sky, blasting Bob off him and sliding across the ring, 'You can't do it, can you? Your species existence is at stake but you can't take my life to save them, oh, this is perfect!'

His jumpsuit damaged and burnt so much that the top ripped open. Getting up and ripping it off he reached into his pocket. He admitted that he did make a very good point.

Using the wind Mr Red blew a gust of sharp air into him, seeing this Bob stepped to the side but the wind sliced open his chest, blood spurting from it and spraying the ground. He grunted and fell to one knee gasping out of exhaustion now.

'Typical, you mortals aren't built for battles such as these,' Mr Red told him sending a kick of air into his face, making a deep cut on his cheek and making him fall to the ground.

Bob grunted as he put one hand to the ground, forcing himself to stand up.

'I don't understand why you keep getting up!'

In a burst of speed Mr Red appeared right next to him, sending a punch into his chin and making him hit the wall face first. Carly kept her eyes on the fight watching Bob getting pummelled on the wall. Mr Red punched him mercilessly, blood spurting everywhere.

She winced once the burning got more intense, right now every mortal was feeling the pain getting worse. Soon they will be nothing but burnt corpses. But she kept her eyes on the fight, praying that Bob will win. 'Come on you can do this,' she said.

Four minutes till the extinction of mortals.

Bob coughed up the blood and fell to the ground. Mr Red standing over him triumphed, 'Look at you, a weak mortal thinking he could take on the gods,' he kicked him to the wall, holding him there and pushed Bob squishing against the flames now, 'This world will be a better place without mortals to destroy everything they touch.'

Bob used his talent to hold himself against the wall refusing to be put through it, for if he goes through it then that's it he's done.

'Give up already!' he yelled pressing against his back now so he can start going into the wall, Bob's fingers feeling the burning hot air outside now and caught fire, 'I am a god to you! Someone who should be feared and worshipped! Without you there will be no one to challenge my RIGHT!'

Feeling his palms going through Bob looked at Carly. She had begun going black seeing the fear in her eyes as the end draws near.

In that moment he thought back to Emma and Wolfe and Carly's family.

'Never again,' he said coldly.

His body levitated into the air slipping out from under Mr Red's foot floating with his talent. 'Impossible,' said Mr Red. Carly recognised it as the same move, Wolfe used back at the prison. Bob spun around and gave a flying electrified fist straight into his face. The impact broke his nose and zapped him back across the ring with Bob standing back up, his fighting spirit stronger than ever.

Mr Red yelled out, getting up he wiped the blood from his face. 'How dare you make me bleed!' he cried out.

Bob charged his entire body with his talent, electricity surging around him like a conduit charged with power. Taking a stance he took a deep breath, 'You call yourself a god, but you are just as evil as any person I met in that hellhole.'

'How dare you compare me to your kind!' Mr Red's body was charged up with red electricity making him fast enough to appear in front of him and sent out a punch, but Bob hit his fist away.

'You are right, I refuse to kill anyone but for you I will make that exception,' Bob told him.

'You cannot kill me!' Mr Red roared using his own electricity to turn his muscles into monstrous sizes while making his chin get thicker along with it. He grew ten times taller than Bob, 'I will use my power to crush you like the insect you are!'

he screamed with all his might thrusting a huge fist charged up right at Bob.

Bob blocked it with his own fist, connecting with it and sent out his own but Mr Red's fist connected as well. They continued sending more punches and blocked each other that at each connection sent out more shockwaves from them. Mr Red sent another at him, with Bob blocking that one, then another and another and another. Soon both were punching at each other with charged up barrages of multiples fists! Each blocking each other but some got a punch in, one punch at Bob one punch at Mr Red, both hitting each other with everything they got.

Carly felt the shockwave flowing through her, not enough to get rid of the fire burning her, of course, but enough to crack the floor around them. She noticed pieces of the walls crumbling down around her, she opened her mouth to speak but she could not, for her mouth was too burnt up to talk! But she knew this fight will take the tower down.

Right now, the whole structure was falling apart, the blows they dealt out making more pieces fall off. The hole in the ceiling was getting bigger and more dangerous with one side of the tower falling down from the side.

She had to get out, not to run away but to not be here when this tower falls. But she could not feel her legs; in fact she could not feel anything then she fell to the ground. She just managed to lift up her head to continue watching. Even if she wasn't burning to a crisp right now, she knew she won't have enough time to get out before this whole place falls.

The people at the ground all burnt in agony, not seeing the tower falling apart like a tower of blocks being knocked over. All around the world mortals were close to seeing the light fade from their eyes, their loved ones who were magic watched in terror; not knowing what is happening but knowing that this was the end.

One minute till the extinction of the mortals.

The punches stopped, both fighters huffing and gasping for air. The end was near and Mr Red knew it, so he chuckled and laughed at the top of his lungs, 'It's over! You are too late!' he laughed mocking Bob for his defeat; the guardian believed that he had won.

Bob did not say a word, only reached into his pocket.

'There is nothing in your pocket that can stop this!' Mr Red mocked, 'Go ahead pull something out I could use a laugh.'

Bob grinned, 'OK, you're the boss mate.'

He grabbed a hold and pulled, electricity surging through his hands all the way from the top of his head. The electricity charged around his cranium powering up his mind and his hands. He began to pull a huge handle out of his pocket and kept on pulling it until he had it in both hands using his talent to hold it up. Mr Red took a step back, widening his eyes at the large item in his hands. 'But… How?' he could only say.

Bob held a giant hammer, the hammer itself gold and lined with magical rubies around it. The handle was woven in ancient runic cloth lined with even more magical runes making it strong enough to resist all kinds of magic. This sort of thing never existed before nor had it been thought of, but Bob imagined it and believed he can pull it out from nowhere; using the talent to supercharge his mind. He created the weapon out of pure thought alone and pulled it out of his pockets, going as far as any taskmaster has ever gone, thanks to combining two talents at the same time. He had literally pulled this straight out of his imagination!

Bob held it up and leaned it back for a final slam; Mr Red will not let him have the chance so he sent gusts of sword like winds into him. But Bob twisted the handle to activate the runes that made a magic shield around him, remembering seeing the exact thing in a video game somewhere. The shield protected him from the winds that would've impaled him.

'IMPOSSIBLE!' yelled Mr Red shaking down to his knees.

Bob slammed his foot down; cracking the ground beneath him he held the handle over his head. Now using all he's got left into this one final strike.

Mr Red stepped back the fear getting to him with the realisation that this is how he is going to die, at the hands of a mortal! 'Do not do this!' He yelled at the top of his lungs, 'I am your god and your master! You don't have the right to do this to ME!'

'Oh god just shut up, already.'

He threw the hammer down like a falling boulder. The weight of the tip helped make it fall faster than Mr Red had ever seen, he screamed once the hammer knocked against the winds that he desperately tried to block with. The Hammer slammed right into his face, knocking him backwards into the ground. The weight of it made his spine and bones burst into splinters, cracking the ground than ever before once he became pressed between them. Soon the ground could not hold it anymore and split open under him, the tower breaking and falling apart around them faster than the fire could reach the air.

Mr Red could not move nor could he do anything. All that power he had but no time to properly think or use them. The light began fading from his eyes, the mortal used his power to create something that can specifically negate his power. He closed his eyes for the final time cursing the mortal who killed him.

The ring of the fire vanished instantly, Bob let go of the hammer and started to fall as well. Carly felt the ground leave her and fell in to the big gaping hole, the fire stopped burning her so she could see clearly, now. Although she did wish to have been burnt, since being a splat on the ground sounded way more painful. She glowed her eyes and called out to any bird to come rescue them, but there weren't any birds around since the battle scared away all the animals from the area. They were so distressed that the animals stole a car to escape so nothing was going to save her.

Then a rock struck her already injured head and she saw nothing.

Carly groaned while she opened her eyes to see the horizon over the sunlit valley.

Looking around at all the soldiers and taskmasters getting to their feet, the fire died down around them as well. Jim was yelling at his men about how they were all wusses for letting a little fire stop them for doing their jobs.

'But sir, you were on fire too,' one taskmaster said, a nice Asian man who was great at making noodles.

'Nonsense, I was smoking a cigarette and had a cancer attack!' Jim yelled back, maintaining his cool.

'That's not how it works, plus, I don't think you smoke.'

Her head felt like a truck ran over it a couple of times. Straining her neck, she looked at herself being carried. Bob was holding her, covered in blood and standing still. 'Got you before you hit the ground,' he said.

Carly turned her head away. 'I did not need your help,' she huffed, 'I could have survived by myself.'

Bob chuckled, setting her down so she could stand on her own.

'So did we win?' she asked looking up at him.

Bob nodded. 'Yeah we won,' he said then fell on his knees then on the ground.

Carly screamed and knelt down, trying to wake him. 'Hey don't you die on me!' she begged shaking him. But she did not get a response, not even a snarky remark, 'Come on Bob!'

'Don't worry girl,' Jim said walking through the rubble towards them. Carly looked up at him, being on the verge of tears. 'He is not dead, just sleeping,' he told her.

Carly took a deep breath. 'Thank god,' she said sitting back on her hands and wiping her eyes.

'Yep, he is out cold,' Jim continued, 'It's understandable seeing as he put up quite a big fight.' He turned back to his men, 'Everyone! The guardians are dead! WE WON!'

All the Taskmasters cheered to the skies. Carly smiled and looked up as well, 'We did it Wolfe, you can now rest in peace.'

Around the world the mortals had stopped burning, in fact they looked like it never happened at all. Families celebrated while sorcerers gave excuses as to why they were suddenly blowing water from their hands. Not a single one of them knew about the fight with the guardians.

Chapter 19

The sounds of tapping fingers filled the office.

Violet groaned. 'Where the hell are they?' she huffed.

It had been five days since the defeat of the guardians. The taskmaster, well, the new taskmaster had been healing up in the medical bay with his apprentice since then, today they were supposed to leave and come straight to her office for a debriefing. She told that prisoner specifically so he won't forget.

But, of course, they never showed up.

Violet tapped the button on the intercom. 'Reception, where the hell is that taskmaster? I was told he left the med bay this morning,' she said in a calm tense voice.

'Um…well, Miss Violet, um… I don't know how to tell you this…' The voice on the box said.

The whole hub shook under the vibrations of her scream, 'HE'S WHERE?!'

'This is a bad idea,' Carly said.

Her and Bob just got out of the med bay and already they were at the pub having a drink. Bob was finally out of his prison jumpsuit but only 'cause there wasn't a spare at the store so he just wore a dirty shirt and orange jeans while Carly wore a hoodie to cover the bandages wrapped around her like a mummy.

The trip to the pub was Jim's treat, of course, for saying thanks for saving their hides. The two sat at the bench waiting for their drinks while Jim gave his thanks and decided to grab them himself.

'You sure, Carla will let you behind there?' Carly asked watching him grabbing the mugs.

'Of course, she can be a hot head but I have special privileges,' he just said handing the drinks out. 'There we go three beers!' he said.

Carly grinned and went to grab her drink but Bob snatched it away from her. 'Jim, she's thirteen,' he said.

'Oh, my mistake,' Jim said grabbing out a tiny umbrella and putting it in her drink, 'There we go.'

'How did you get your job again?' Carla said behind him. She grabbed her towel and smacked him a couple of times to get him away from the bench. 'I catch you here again and you will be circumcised!' she threatened.

Then she took back the drink, also taking Carly's grin.

Jim took a seat next to them. 'Eh, I never liked handing out drinks anyway,' he said taking a sip of his beer.

Carla handed Carly a glass of coke cola. 'On the house,' she told her.

Carly thanked her and took a sip, 'OK, everyone!' Jim called out getting up on the bench, 'I would like us all to take a moment of silence, sure we won against a very powerful enemy but we also lost a great man along the way,' the whole pub fell silent, 'John Wolfe was one of our best, when we all had our toughest times we could count on him to give us a hand, he was a great friend and a great taskmaster.'

Carly nodded while getting teary eyed so she quickly wiped them away. Bob just faced ahead.

'We shall remember him and his kindness, so let's all have a minute of silence for Taskmaster, Wolfe,' Jim finished raising his mug soon followed by everyone raising theirs, along with Carly and yes even Bob.

They hung in silence for a solid minute then all took a drink.

'Now let's all get crazy drunk!' Jim bellowed chugging down the rest of his drink along the cheers of the soldiers.

Carly could not help but laugh at this but she suddenly got a chill on the back of her neck, 'So there you idiots are,' she turned to see Violet standing in the doorway. Everyone spat out their drinks and coughed while she walked through them towards Bob and Carly.

Jim nearly choked on his beer, 'Violet! I thought you were too busy with Haven work,' he said getting off the bench.

'Who told you that,' she said. Jim hesitated and glanced at Bob. 'So, I see,' she said pushing him away and going up to him. She folded her arms, 'We had a meeting today.'

Bob looked back at her. 'Yeah, I know,' he said.

'So why did you not come to my office? The reception desk told me you went straight to the pub instead.'

'Are you serious?' Carly whispered glaring at Bob.

Bob sighed and turned around, leaning back on the bench, 'I just did not bother showing up, you are just going to be annoying.'

Jim awkwardly and slowly moves towards the door along with everyone else. Soon the whole pub became empty except for Violet, Bob and Carly.

'You have some nerve,' she said, 'After I made you a taskmaster and this is how you repay me, give me one good reason why I shouldn't strip you of your rank and kick you out of here?'

'Because you want to keep me,' Bob said, 'I have two talents and have the power to create god killer weapons at my disposal, you want to use someone like me, so I don't think you would kick out your top weapon.'

Violet smirked, 'Smart guy, alright you got me there but I will be keeping my eye on you,' she said.

'Gotcha is that all?'

'No in fact,' she took a seat with them, 'The extinction spell did not go unnoticed, around the world all the magical communities are investigating, lucky we have covered our tracks so well,' she added, 'What with no one seeming to have noticed the guardians are missing and they aren't brave enough to go check.'

'But there's a downside,' Carly said.

Violet ignored her, 'On their investigations, our people on the inside discovered they used psychics to find the culprit and guess who they saw,' she pointed to Bob, 'They all saw your face so they will be coming after you.'

Now it is Bob's turn to grin, 'Let them come,' he said.

Soon Bob and Carly left the pub, walking along the pathway towards the building they were staying at for a while.

'So am I going to expect you to do really insane stuff like that? You're lucky she did not chuck us in gaol!' she yelled at him.

'As if she has the guts,' Bob said.

Carly looked at him, 'So aren't you worried?'

'About?'

'Sorcerers coming after you, well, coming after us since I'm stuck with you until I become a taskmaster,' she added putting her hands behind her head.

Bob turned to her, 'So you decided to stay as my apprentice?' he asked.

'Well, face it without me to show you the ropes you would be lost in our little secret, secret world,' she said with a slight giggle.

'Smart aleck.'

Carly smiled, 'Honestly, I'm glad to have you around; after all I need someone who is second best to teach me.'

'Second best, now?'

'Yeah, Wolfe was the best but now I'm stuck with someone who doesn't even know what he's doing half the time.'

Bob chuckled, 'That crazy old man always messing with me even after death.'

Carly laughs, annoying Bob even more as the two heroes walked towards the hanger doors.

They started out as an unlikely team but through the battles and through the trials, losses and victories, they both now considered each other as a family, and Carly wouldn't have it any other way. So now here they go, off to a new adventure.

Chapter 20

The remains of the tower lay still under the dark moonlit sky.

Violet walked along the rocks and rubbles, admiring the damage that caused this great tower to fall. Wrapped in her fur coat for she hated the cold Australian air. 'Where is that prick,' she mumbled.

Soon, she spotted him. A man no older than his early forties walked up to her, a gentleman wearing a nice dark red suit that gleamed in the moonlight.

'I hate to say it but your stupid prophecy worked,' Violet said.

'The guardians believed it enough that it led to their downfall,' she put a cigarette in her mouth and lit it.

The man smiled. 'I told you that it would,' he said.

'Oh, yeah, except the part about some complete stranger taking the role of taskmaster.'

'I admit he was unexpected, you are keeping an eye on him?'

Violet took a puff, 'Of course, I figured so he doesn't go and screw up our plan.'

The man said nothing only looking up at the night sky, 'Now that the guardians are gone, we can finally go ahead without any fear of being found out,' she continued, 'Now we have to deal with the Magical Community.'

He nodded then finally said, 'How is she by the way, my daughter?'

Violet looked at him, 'Oh Carly is growing up just fine.'